The World, The Lizard and Me

For France-Isabelle

The World, The Lizard and Me

Gil Courtemanche

Translated by David Homel

SEREN
DISCOVERIES

Seren is the book imprint of
Poetry Wales Press Ltd
Nolton Street, Bridgend, Wales

www.serenbooks.com
facebook.com/SerenBooks
Twitter: @SerenBooks

Original French text © Gil Courtemanche, 2010
Translation © David Hamel, 2015

First published in Québécois by Éditions du Boréal, 2009

ISBN 978-1-78172-265-7
Mobi: 978-1-78172-272-5
Epub: 978-1-78172-279-4

A CIP record for this title is available from
the British Library

The publisher works with the financial assistance
of the Welsh Books Council

Printed by Pulsio, Paris, France

Cover Artwork:
Adaption of 'Childs play' by Nelson de Witt (CC BY 2.00), and 'Kids
come out, Summer has arrived' by Josh Pesavento (CC BY-SA 2.0).

This translation is published with the support of the Centre National
du Livre

Avec le soutien du

www.centrenationaldulivre.fr

The World, The Lizard and Me

1

Bunia obsesses me. It's just a little town, a hole, a cross-roads I never set foot in. No-one knows the place in the eastern Congo. But the way an archaeology student knows the Acropolis by heart, or the pyramids of Cheops without having visited them, I know this town. It's my world. I've been studying and analysing the history of Bunia for the last three years: the murders committed there, the alliances, the armed factions, the criminals who dominated the place, the ethnic divisions, the economic activities, the major landowners, the smuggling networks.

I am one of the world's few Bunia specialists. I know the composition of the soil, the flora and fauna, the anarchic occupation of the land. I could give a seminar about Bunia. I know the trails as if I'd travelled them myself, the ones that lead to the diamonds and gold and coltan. I know the price of the staples from last week's market. I've read the menu at the restaurant at the Hotel Bunia where the cheese comes from Vietnam – a strange and intriguing touch, since the owner is a Kurdish refugee. I even know the first names of the handful of prostitutes who hang out at the bar. According to one blog, Madeleine will do absolutely anything. Another blog written by an American evangelical missionary suggests the reader avoid the place entirely. That's where we are going to live for several days. What can Vietnamese cheese taste like?

I'll be getting there Tuesday, via Nairobi and Entebbe, with Pascal and Claus. I'm anxious and a little overwrought, like before a first date or a final exam, and

I try in vain to relax at the bar at the hotel I'm living in, where I'm watching the Euro 2008 match between Holland and France. A few Dutchmen have started hollering, and the game hasn't even started. I imagine Bunia, I'm inventing it, but I'm sure I won't be surprised. One hundred thousand people, three hotels, a Lebanese restaurant, one that's more or less Italian, and a Greek one. I know the history of the town better than the people who live there. I know everything without ever having been there. All that's missing now is to walk the streets, smell the smells, eat, and talk with the people I've been analyzing for the last three years. I've never felt the need because my files are complete and exhaustive, my information channels myriad, and here, at the Court, we don't work with impressions and feelings, we use tools of scientific analysis. That's my job, and I love it. It satisfies me completely. Until now, I always preferred discovering the world through books, reports, and studies. This approach allows for an independence of mind and objectivity necessary to the jurists we are.

A magnificent goal by van Nistelrooy, 1-0 for Holland. An extraordinary header after a corner kick. The French don't give in to desperation and that encourages me. They attack intelligently and, though it's not exactly their trademark, with some intensity. I forget all about Bunia for a few minutes. A Dutchman falls off his stool and curses out the furniture. I think of Bunia after all.

Bunia is a city that fell off its stool one day, whipped up by nationalist and ethnic intoxication, or so it says in the NGO reports. The Dutchman quarrels with his stool and loses the battle when the Orangemen make it 2-0. His friends are shouting even louder, and one of them pours a pint of Heineken on his head. Uglier than ugliness itself, he is choking, lying on the floor like a drunk pig, and with animal grunts he begins vomiting. The customers burst out laughing except for me, the staff, and two or three respectable Dutchmen who head for their rooms. Sometimes Dutch behaviour shocks their more puritanical compatriots. I decided to go up to my room. I think of Bunia as Holland humiliates France. When the assistant prosecutor announced I was leaving for Bunia, I asked why. Weren't my analyses satisfactory? They were perfect and had established the bases of the accusations brought against Thomas Kabanga, the leader of the Congolese Patriotic Union. This Bunia militiaman in Ituri, a province of the Congo, will be the first to be judged by the International Criminal Court. The trial will write a new page of international justice and judge a new crime, the forced enrolment of child soldiers. Kabanga is not an elected official; he is more like a loading dock. He is involved wherever diamonds, gold and coltan are trafficked. Coltan fascinates me. It's a mineral that can be harvested like potatoes, by scratching the surface of the earth, and it is used to make iPods, BlackBerrys, and smartphones. The hills of Ituri help us live less and communicate more.

Kabanga takes his share off the customs checkpoints, and deals with the Lebanese mafia. He's a sort of facilitator, a go-between, a bridge. He's the link with the Rwanda of President Kagamé who manipulates everything. Child soldiers work for him. You have to understand what it was like back then: six foreign armies were carving up the Congo at the beginning of the twenty-first century. In Ituri, the Ugandans were running the show. Kabanga made contact with them. He became the supplier of beans for Kampala's troops, and they encouraged him to develop the nationalism of the Hema, his ethnic group, against the Lendu.

The Court thought I was in the best position to gauge

the reaction of Bunia's population to the trial. "Don't you want to see if what you've been writing is true, true in concrete terms?" I had never asked myself that question. "Don't you think that touching and smelling and seeing might help you?" The Court assistant was right. He'd eaten grilled goat in Africa, caught malaria at age twenty-seven, and drunk more Primus in three years than the number of beers I'd had in my entire life. He was right, but we were different. I was running from life, like a pupil who understands nothing of the mysterious mutations of biology. I preferred mathematics and statistics. The realm of the measurable was comforting, but the idea of testing my three years of reflection with a reality check did seem logical.

I knew very little of Africa from personal experience. A mission for an NGO in the Ivory Coast when I was a neophyte. I never saw a man from the Ivory Coast pour a glass of beer on a friend's head. I never saw a man from the Ivory Coast vomit in a bar and laugh about it.

But I did know Africa very well. I could talk about the place for hours, for days. When we sit down to a meal that is supposed to be convivial, my few friends often suggest I keep my opinions to myself. I write reports, sophisticated analyses, mostly about the region of the Great Lakes and the Darfur. I don't have a naïve, complacent view of Africa. I compile lists of murders and massacres, study accusations of cannibalism, explore the trafficking in diamonds, and wide-scale rape. I produce documents concerning the secret finances of heads of state and leaders of various militias, their ties to international mafias and mining companies listed on the stock exchanges in New York and Toronto. Memos about the contraband in gold and coltan. I compile detailed reports from Doctors Without Borders that describe sexual violence and rape in the territories that concern me. I live my life in the midst of violence that is written, documented, and often photographed, but the most violent act I have witnessed was the Dutchman vomiting at the bar I've been going to for the last three years.

My name is Claude Tremblay, and for the last three years, I've been a political analyst for the office of the Chief Prosecutor at the International Criminal Court in The Hague.

All my colleagues rent apartments in The Hague and Amsterdam. I chose a hotel in the dreary suburb of Voorburg, a few minutes from The Hague. Sometimes I wonder if a normal life, with love, children, and time off can be reconciled with such extraordinary work. When your responsibility is to unmask and issue documents to arrest and bring to trial war criminals, true monsters, men who defy every international law and convention, do you have the right to a normal life and to take time off from the task at hand? I don't believe so, even if I respect and sometimes envy those people who prefer a woman, or man, and children, and switch off their mobile phones when they leave the horrible white tower in which the Court is housed. I don't consider myself any purer than they are, since my solitude agrees with me and suits me. To do my work, I have decided to live differently than my colleagues. I am at peace with my solitude; it lets me immerse myself completely in the lives of the victims of the crimes I describe so minutely that sometimes the prosecutor is horrified.

"I don't need those terrible details."

"Yes, sir, but they are the most important ones."

"I don't need to know about the lit cigar in the anus."

"Yes, you do."

"I suppose you have a photo?"

"Yes. I can show it to you."

I live in the Hotel Mövenpick, a Swiss Holiday Inn, patronized by business travellers, accountants, and sometimes Court consultants. The staff is uninterested in me, and the heavy, impassive waitresses sometimes give me a half-smile. Since I've been in Holland, I have neglected the culinary refinement my parents taught me. The Swiss-Dutch approximation of gastronomy doesn't bother me, and neither does the pasta at Il Pomodoro, a pizzeria whose Italian owners display a more kindly approach to me than the Dutch. We agree on this on those evenings when I allow myself a glass of wine after a *pizza di Parma*, the best I've eaten in my entire life. My ex-wife, Nathalie, laughed at me when I sent her a rare e-mail containing the recipe. She wasn't making fun of the pizza; she was mocking my enthusiasm. "There's nothing more exciting in your life than a Dutch pizza?"

Nathalie never understood my passion for justice, and that led to our separation. I didn't feel the need to answer, and return to what had made her so unhappy and me so alone, a prisoner in a room for the last three years, in a mediocre suburb of a mediocre city.

Four to one for Holland. I feel a twinge of regret. I like France well enough, especially Brittany, where once every three months I allow myself time off from my work as an analyst of horror. During those weekends I do nothing. I don't visit the museums. I eat what I used to in my parents' house: kidneys, hanger steak, and sweet-breads. Those things bring back good memories, untouched by nostalgia. I drink a small amount of good wine, I envy people's apparently carefree nature, but I don't forget my work. When I return to Voorburg, I do so with guilty feelings: I have neglected my passion, as if I had betrayed a woman I more than loved – I idolized.

I rarely try to explain my passion for justice. That passion seems irrational and naïve, like a teenager who believes in a better world even as he watches scenes of violence on TV instead of looking at music videos. I love music, almost all kinds. Music transports me, it makes me greater than I am. I don't have a very high opinion of myself. I'm neither handsome nor ugly, and no more intelligent than the average. Once I had some success with a girl who briefly became my wife until my work took up too much room. I'm alone, but no more so than my friends who are part of a couple. That suits me and, I believe, helps me in my work, since nothing interferes and takes my mind off the violence and inhumanity that I chronicle for the Court. If I apply myself, if I build an exemplary and detailed case, my work can lead to a field investigation that will bring a war criminal to justice. And that's no mean feat for a thirty-five-year-old Montreal man who, when he was eleven, knew nothing of the world outside of the postcards his parents sent from their Paris vacations, and a globe won in a geography contest, the strange names of a few countries, and an immigrant and his two children who went to school with him. I knew they came from Africa (all Blacks come from Africa), but we never talked much. It wasn't racism, just indifference mixed in with the need to be wary of others.

I was a little shy, more than I am now, and I didn't like talking much, afraid I might say something silly and be laughed at. I know now that I feared rejection and criticism. The comfort of the standards and rules handed down by my parents protected me, and I was particularly uneasy when a teacher who subscribed to liberation pedagogy, a bearded, slovenly man who dressed the way students weren't allowed to, asked us to improvise on the theme of our 'daily life.'

"Claude, let's say your mother slaps you for the wrong reason. You're not guilty of the mistake she says you made. I'll play your mother and you react."

"My mother never slaps me."

"But let's imagine something impossible. Your mother slaps you and calls you a liar."

"Sir, that's too impossible for me to imagine."

With an angry look, my mother asked me why I got a bad grade in oral expression since, according to her, I expressed myself better than most students. I told her about the improvisation exercise and she kissed me on the forehead, a kiss longer and warmer than usual. It proved I was right to respect the rules and codes that the people I loved and respected had set down for me, for my future.

I was eleven years old when the world's disorder entered my mind and took up position next to the moral and family codes I had been given and respected without feeling constrained.

My parents chose to protect me from the world's evil. They avoided all discussions of politics when I was around and turned off the television when the news came on. I knew only fragments about the mafia, war, conflicts, and natural disasters. I vaguely sensed that such things existed, but they stayed far from my peaceful universe, and I was sheltered from them forever – or until the teachers went on strike and picketed in front of the main door of the school to make sure no one got in.

It's not easy to explain to a child the meaning of 'End Exploitation' and 'No More Wage Slavery.' My mother said that it was all very complicated and I'd understand when I was older, but that the teachers were good people who should be respected. My father, a civil servant, agreed without bothering to tell me that once he had taken part in a long illegal strike. After a few days, it felt like I was on vacation, going to bed late and getting up later.

On the evening of December 6, 1984, I was alone in the living room reading *Robinson Crusoe* while my parents were busy outside, protecting the ornamental plants and bushes that beautified the front of the house against the coming winter. I turned on the television. I heard outraged shouting, crying and barking, death rattles and sounds I had never heard before. A round hut like the ones I had seen in geography books. All around were hundreds of fragile shelters made of stakes set in triangular fashion, covered with canvas or animal skins, I couldn't tell which. In each tent that opened onto a burning sun, Black people were prostrate as if in prayer. They were holding small children in their arms. The camera entered the hut and circled the interior. A dozen naked children were lying on the ground. I didn't hear what the journalist was saying, I stared astonished at the bodies as thin as sticks, their ribs like the skeleton of a picked over fish, their cheeks hollow like holes bored in their faces, and black eyes that stared into a distance I could not imagine. I thought it was the sun. Hands that hung at the end of long skinny arms took hold of a child and set him in a hollowed out tree trunk filled with water. Hands washed the child who stared at the sun, painfully thin hands placed the child on a blanket on a bed of leaves and branches. I closed my eyes and my ears opened: "This is the fifty-fourth death in Bati and it's not even noon." Those children weren't sleeping, they were dead. How, why? And where was Bati? I turned off the television and ran into my room. I had just seen children dying of hunger in an African country. That was all I understood, but for my modest knowledge of the world, it was too much. I wasn't on the same planet anymore. My parents had described a world with codes and laws and rules founded on respect and civility. In that world, no child died of hunger. In the one I'd just wandered into, it seemed that death, for children, was a normal event. The journalist had spoken of Ismail who was eleven years old, my age, an eleven-year-old version of me who died of hunger. As I tried to fall asleep, I searched for the words and the way to let my parents know they should have told me about this other planet. All I could think of was, "Ismail was eleven like me and he died of hunger." In that depth of insomnia, I found this question: "Where is Bati?" And when I awoke, still tormented: "Do you know what's happening in the world away from here?" It was my apprenticeship of insomnia. Adolescence was over before it began.

The next morning, I remembered, "Ismail was eleven like me and he died of hunger." I arrived at the breakfast table in a terrible state, with those words on my lips.

Father put his newspaper on the table, and Mother, who was fixing eggs, came and sat down. From their questioning silence, and their eyes that fell upon me like teachers ready to reprimand, I felt they understood that an important event had occurred in my life. They waited patiently for me to tell them. I spat it out in no particular order: the fifty children, the bodies washed and set out on eucalyptrus branches. "Eucalyptus," my father corrected me, waiting for what would come next. Nothing came next. Mother served the eggs. Father returned to his paper.

After ten days of questions about Africa and the teachers' strike, I learned that a famine was raging in Ethiopia, that probably one or two million people had starved to death, that no one knew why, that it was no doubt due to a drought, that yes, we were rich, but the teachers thought they were poorly paid, and that we couldn't do anything for the people of Ethiopia, or the teachers. 'We' – that was my parents and me. After ten days of persistent questions, and my parents having exhausted all their answers that didn't really answer anything, they let me watch the TV news, probably hoping to get free of my full-time, obsessive inquisition. "Why is Africa so poor and why are we so rich?" No answer. "Why don't we jail the rich who could save the poor but don't?"

The first day back at school after the strike ended, I asked my teacher if he was poor. No, of course not, he said, but poverty is relative. "Then why did you go on strike?" It was for the quality of education, he told me. Mr. Nantel continued droning on in his nasal voice and he bought a new car the next month. For the rest of the year, he managed to turn me off mathematics. I forgot the sciences too. I'd do something more human. What would that be? No idea. Before I could choose, I'd need to know the world better.

2

Now I know our lives evolve sometimes like the great spring tides of the Brittany coast. One morning, on the first day of a new phase of life, the Bay of Paimpol is empty, as dry as if the sea had never been there. Alone, in the middle, a thin trickle of water reminds us it was once a bay and that the sea knew it. Then the water, like a painter working in successive layers of colour, covers the sand and the beach with a blue tinted by the sand it barely laps at. The progress continues for days, which for a bay emptied of its water must be the equivalent of years for a man. Water takes its place. At the beginning of the spring tide, the oysters lined up in rows on their trellis suffer from the sun and lack of water. Their thirst grows ever more powerful and, as the water becomes more generous, they gorge themselves eagerly. People say, though no one believes it, that spring tide oysters are the fleshiest, that their salt taste is more refined, and their iodine content higher than the oysters born of ordinary tides. As for the bay, after two weeks, it awakens so full of water it sometimes grazes rocks never touched by the sea. Now that I was allowed to discover the world, I resembled a pebble or an oyster raised and nourished by the great spring tides.

My eleventh summer was a studious one, to the dismay of my parents who wanted me to be different from them – active and athletic. I loved sports, especially tennis and hockey, and I was good at both. Paradoxically, my parents, even as they encouraged me to play those sports, denigrated professional athletes and the amorphous cohort of their fans. Once my father said,

"Sports is the new opium of the people." He was talking about professional sports, which were very far from my mind, but it was obvious he couldn't reconcile his desire to see me strong and agile with his fear that I would really get interested in sports and want to pursue them seriously. Without realizing it, my parents oriented me in a different direction.

After the right to watch the TV news, I was given the right to read my father's paper. For my birthday, I received books that weren't adventure novels for once: atlases with commentary, a work on Native American culture, and the 1985 *Yearbook*.

I never knew there were so many countries. I'd been told how many continents there were, and that was deemed sufficient. The writing was much too complicated. The articles discussed GNPs and growth rates, types of government and education status. I decided to begin at the beginning: I'd learn the names of the countries, continent by continent, and the capital cities, and then the population of each country. I wondered which ones were rich and which poor. I read that the growth rate for Ethiopia was 8% in 1984. If that was true, why had I watched a boy my age starving to death? Father must know. "One day I'll explain, Claude." I didn't push any further, but his refusal to answer intrigued me, especially because he read the newspaper voraciously, along with books on political subjects, and sometimes I caught him telling Mother that the world was essentially rotten.

We lived in a comfortable, well-off neighbourhood. Every house had its backyard. Our Greek, Italian, and Portuguese neighbours generally covered theirs in asphalt. The French-speaking ones grew gardens decorated with typical flowers, geraniums and pansies, sometimes a few fuchsias. Our neighbours grew tomatoes and cucumbers on the bit of land that separated the houses from the sidewalk. We planted ferns and wide-leaved plants. My mother drew inspiration from traditional Japanese gardens, she said. The neighbours, no matter their relation to cucumbers or fuchsias, got along wonderfully. They stood together on the sidewalk and talked, they invited each other in for a drink, and the Italian lady always made sure we tasted her first tomatoes. When summer came, the dynamic of the encounters changed, as did the smoke that each yard breathed out. Barbecues were trotted out and invitations flowed. A primitive scent filled the air, the smell of grilling meat, sputtering fat, and vegetables that blackened over flames that were too high, a wild odour of the country, the savannah, foreign essences. Father considered that the barbecue ritual was bourgeois, but he never hesitated when an invitation was involved. With the Greeks, he talked for hours about the Colonels, with the Portuguese, the month of April, with the Italians, the Red Brigades. He seemed to know everything about the world, or at least about these countries, though he never smiled during these long conversations. Chewing on a sausage, he looked sombre and preoccupied, then he would set down his uneaten plate of shish kebabs and launch into an endless tirade. He seemed to have codes and keys and tools to explain the world he kept from me.

When Mother announced that she had bought a barbecue, "an ordinary one," and that it was time to invite our neighbours, my father sighed. "Have we really gotten that bourgeois? A barbecue party!" It wasn't one of those gas models that were taking over the backyards of the neighbourhood, but a kind of black pit in which you piled real charcoal or wood briquettes and laboured to light.

"How come you don't like barbecues, and what does 'bourgeois' mean?"

"Let me explain. Your mother and I haven't always lived this way. A bourgeois… that's someone who's satisfied with himself and wants to defend his place in society. Someone who obeys society's codes."

I was reassured, at least partly. I wasn't satisfied with myself and I had no place in society. But we always scrupulously respected its codes.

I had a methodical mind that took nothing for granted, and that included what my father said. When I opened the dictionary to look for 'bourgeois', I realized I was becoming myself by not being satisfied with his evasive answers. The demand to watch television was the first step in my rebellion, and searching the dictionary was the beginning of my independence.

Such things might seem banal. A child methodically taking control of his life, with neither anger nor rejection, setting down his foundations. Those are my nostalgic thoughts as I watch an insipid French series on TV, in a Swiss hotel in a dismal suburb of a monotonous city. I hear the 11:59 pulling into the station. My window is always open and the trains help me tell time. I know the schedules of every train going to Rotterdam and Gouda, even the ones that don't stop in Voorburg. The 11:59 comes from Utrecht.

Sometimes, even for those of us who have chosen it, solitude can become intolerable. We fill it imperfectly by sending messages in a bottle. These days, the man who has lost his way can use e-mail to express his dismay in rapid fashion. He types out, Hi, how are you, haven't heard from you for a while, how's my nephew doing? The people who receive these bottles that are all but empty are surprised by the sudden return of a man who had been totally absent. Sometimes they answer. I sent a few messages and I'm awaiting a response, any kind will do, as long as I can feel I'm not totally alone. There is one new message.

"The Bunia mission is cancelled for security reasons. More tomorrow."

All those vaccinations for nothing. Still stuck in Voorburg.

Then another message, an answer to one of my bottles from Nathalie, my ex-wife. "If you're writing, you must really be alone. I'm doing fine, I'm happy in love and, you couldn't know it, but I'm pregnant. We moved into a nice apartment in the same part of town as your parents. A little garden, a parasol, lounge chairs, friendly neighbours. Do you still think we can change the world? I hope you're not too unhappy."

No, I'm not too unhappy. I chose this life and, in part thanks to my work, Thomas Kabanga, the criminal of Bunia, will soon be tried and found guilty. Thousands of anonymous, voiceless victims, with no means of defending themselves, will finally be granted justice. And that's no mean feat. I liked Nathalie well enough, but I travelled the world through books, and she liked her cafés and her friends who chattered about everything and nothing. I preferred to talk about everything, and never about nothing.

3

'Bourgeois'. Originally from the French *bourg*, a town-dweller, a person of middle rank in society, as of the shopkeeping class; hence, any person of the middle class. Among radical socialists, a person with private property interests. For a certain Mr. Marx, whom I did not know and who invented communism, the bourgeois exploits the population and constitutes an obstacle to the proletarian revolution.

As a teenager, I read a little Marx, enough to understand how absolute the exploitation of some men by other men was in Russia during his life. But I had trouble with democratic centralism and surplus value.

"Father, do men still exploit other men? What's democratic centralism and why does Marx talk about the freedom of the workers when they're not free in the Communist countries?"

He lowered his copy of *Le Devoir*. He would never have read *La Presse* or *Le Journal de Montréal*.

"Can't you get interested in subjects that are right for your age?"

"Why are there so many books by Marx and Lenin on your shelves?"

"They were for university."

He disappeared behind his newspaper again as Mother gently chided him for not satisfying his son's intellectual curiosity.

What were the subjects right for my age? I was supposed to study, of course, but I didn't feel I was learning anything about the world and how it worked.

Of course there was sports. I played hockey and tennis

with a kind of methodical passion, looking for ways to improve not necessarily my success, but my technical abilities, refining my game and being inventive. Even if I didn't win the point, I was satisfied with my slicing backhand, a difficult shot that landed a few centimetres past the baseline. My adversary won the exchange, but I knew I had perfectly executed the manoeuvre. Victory interested me, but it was always secondary to the quality of my game. The coaches criticized me; I didn't have what it took to win. "Your game is perfect, but you don't have the killer instinct."

I kept on playing, working on my drop shots and my forehands against the back wall of the house. I set up a goalie's net with a piece of plywood behind it, and cut four holes in the four corners of the net. I didn't waste my time practicing slap shots; they were too inaccurate, vulgar shots with a certain pretentious aspect. I worked only on my wrist shot and my backhand.

My methodical approach to sports paid off. I might not have had the killer instinct, but on the court and on the rink, I became a quality player. Not the best, since the best had the killer instinct as well as technique. But doing well in an honourable fashion brought me satisfaction and happiness.

The right subjects for my age? The first video games were coming on the market. They were forbidden in my house, of course. My first cigarette? I smoked it at fifteen. I've been smoking ever since. The first beer came with the first cigarette, but I didn't go too far with either. I was more and more obsessed with poverty, injustice, inequality, and politics – not in my country, but in faraway places. Still, I was an ordinary teenager.

And then there were girls. Of course, girls. My father was worried because I didn't have a girlfriend. He kept making jokes about sex and quizzing me about my experiences that added up to zero. Mother blushed, but he pushed on. "Don't tell me that at age fifteen you haven't kissed a girl yet, and that you've never dreamed of making love. Don't tell me it doesn't keep you up at night, and that you don't feel the need, if you know what I mean, for some release." Mother told him, "You're going too far." If he got some enjoyment out if it, I didn't mind if he made fun of me, since he talked so rarely about subjects that interested me and didn't seem to get much pleasure out of life. I answered him honestly, without feeling diminished because I had no sexual experience, and not much desire for it either. Of course that wasn't completely true. For my research into poverty around the world, I spent time reading dictionaries, and once I came up with my answers, I would turn the pages and linger over the photos. I read the biographies of famous men, complete unknowns to me. I took notes and wrote down the titles of books I should read, and sometimes I gazed at reproductions of classical paintings. I remember Botticelli's *Venus* and a nude by Ingres. The shape of women's breasts, hips, and buttocks was a delight to me. So many gentle, harmonious curves! I never imagined that a woman's body could be so beautiful.

As I listened to my father trying to provoke me, I decided it would be enough to contemplate beauty, and I admit that I watched my mother and tried to imagine her breasts and buttocks. I never thought of touching or caressing. Television, the playground, and locker room conversations between the guys after a game told me all I needed to know about acts and techniques. In that world as well, I was methodical. To look and admire might lead to the desire to touch and all those other mysterious things like kisses with the tongue, the languorous moaning of women, caressing their breasts and then between their legs, and, finally, penetration. I knew about everything, but I had to start by looking so as not to miss a single step of desire. I'd read that love did not exist without desire. I wanted love, so I had to pass through desire.

4

Several years later, at college, I made the acquaintance of Bernard Lafontaine. He was not your everyday sort of professor. At the end of the 1980s, the fashion for teachers was to be scruffy enough to imitate the students, with the same casual manner and the same dirty clothes. Mr. Lafontaine, since he insisted we call him Mister, wore a suit and tie, kept his hair short, and used impeccable grammar. He tolerated no exceptions to proper behaviour, and spoke for forty-five minutes running. "No, I don't have class notes. You take notes; I don't." He taught Morality: The Science of Right and Wrong, a class that everyone hated, but that fascinated me. How do we separate good and evil, justice from injustice, guilt from responsibility? What are rights and what are obligations, and what is the relation between the two? Obviously, Mr. Lafontaine was the most unloved teacher at the college. I figured he knew as much, and didn't care. I admired his indifference because it was a little like my own unconcern with my reputation among the girls and most of my classmates. I would have preferred to be liked, but that wasn't part of my priorities. I did what I needed to do, in my own way, without offending anyone.

I was fascinated by the way he developed opposing theses, systematically refusing to allow his personal preferences to intrude. As I wrote my paper on individual responsibility in society, I spent hours asking myself about my own behaviour with my parents, my friends, in public, and in the stores I went to.

Yes, I was responsible for each of my actions, and any one of them could upset the fragile balance that made it possible for us to live together. But I explained in my paper that this sense of responsibility must not stifle my individuality and my principles, and that personal indignation could also exist and manifest itself.

Mr. Lafontaine rewarded me with an almost perfect grade, and asked me to respond to this question: "How far can we go to change an unjust society?"

Father was talking about the new deck. He wanted a table made of real teak. "We've got the money to buy one, Rosanne." Mother thought teak was too expensive, and conspicuous too, but she gave in to his final argument: "I've gotten my ass chewed off in a shitty job for the last fifteen years, and if I want teak, that's what I'm damned well going to buy. Shit!"

"When we bought the barbecue, you told me you couldn't believe we'd gone that bourgeois. So teak for an outside table..."

"Sure, damn it, we're bourgeois, we've got the money. If you don't like it, you can start the revolution."

Mother obviously had no desire to start any revolution, even with a small "r." "All right," she said softly, and went back to her *osso buco*.

"Rosanne, I'm going down to the cellar. What do you want, a Barolo or a Montepulciano?"

I knew nothing about wine, though on a regular basis, Father would pour me a small glass of this or that, and explain the provenance, the particular zones and territories, the bouquet, the aroma, and the spices. He knew all about wine and would organize tastings with friends and colleagues. They discussed each wine with the same passion I mustered to talk about world poverty with a new girl. I was fine with a bottle of Coke.

This time it was a Barolo, and Father explained its qualities to me, though they went over my head. On the other hand, the veal shanks were a masterpiece.

"Father, how far can we go to change an unjust society?"

"What society are you talking about?"

"Any unjust society."

"Injustice is a relative notion."

"No. Injustice is injustice."

Now I know why, but on the day of *osso buco* and Barolo, I didn't understand why my father got up from the table and declared, "Rosanne, I'm not hungry and I need to see my friends." I went to my room, determined to answer the question, and I didn't notice until later that Mother had finished the bottle of Barolo. She was lying on the sofa in the living room, an empty glass in her hand, snoring. I didn't know women snored.

As Mother was drinking alone, I wrote that the struggle against injustice should know no limits, that all injustices were the same, and, recalling something Martin Luther King had said, I added that the duty of every citizen was to oppose unjust laws. I liked what I had written, and concluded by saying that if violence constituted the only means to fight injustice, then we should not hesitate to turn to violent action and terrorism. I went to bed, drunk on my own words as if I had finished the bottle of Barolo. What did I know about violence? I had never been in a fight, I'd been slapped, and checked into the boards in hockey in a particularly nasty way a few times. When it came to terrorism, I hadn't yet understood that the word that stood at its heart was "terror." I couldn't get to sleep. I was coming down from the excesses of my words. I didn't seriously believe that violence should be used and bombs planted because the levels of welfare payments were unfair. Sweating, I got up and rewrote my conclusion. I dropped the word terrorism and kept the recourse to violence, but only when all other means – political struggle and civil disobedience – failed. Then I fell into a deep sleep.

Father didn't want to read what I had written the next morning. He was hung over, which didn't keep him from reading every single line of the paper, grunting the entire time and exclaiming, "Asshole!" between two sips of coffee.

"I can give you a summary. I'd just like to have your opinion."

"I've told you a thousand times that politics don't interest me anymore. They're all liars and assholes. We have to learn to get along without the idea-peddlers and slogan-mongers."

I was sure that Father was hiding something, but I wasn't the kind to pursue it. Why else would he read *Le Devoir*, since the paper talked about nothing but politics and the economy, if he wasn't interested in those things? In a box in the basement, I'd found *The Communist Manifesto, Left-Wing Communism: An Infantile Disorder*, works by Bakunin, poems written by Rosa Luxemburg, and a few issues of a magazine called *Worker's Forum*. But I settled for the comfort of this explanation because I loved my family: no doubt my parents were protecting me from the world's cruelty and injustice. I would have preferred discovering those things little by little in their company, benefiting from their life experience and wisdom, but I had to travel that path alone, in my own way, aware that it might bring me to believe, if only for a few hours, that terrorism could be justified in a society like ours.

His refusal to get interested in anything that impassioned me gradually unravelled the bond between us. Up till then he had been the ideal father. Always available, never complacent, strict but fair. During my methodical and monotonous acquisition of the techniques of hockey and tennis, he played goalie, defenseman, or opposing winger on the nearby rink. Like a servant in a rich man's club, he positioned himself by the net with a pail full of balls and threw them in my direction. He never missed one of my games, or a parents' meeting, and he instilled in me the proper use of language which allowed me, through books, to discover and understand what sort of world I lived in.

That was how, like the slowly flowing spring tide, quiet but powerful, my relation with my father changed. The shape of our existences began to shift. Once we'd lived together, but now, I lived in his house; he had his life and I was building mine. Respect and affection replaced admiration and love. You might think the experience was painful, but that wasn't how I saw it. Everything happened quietly, with no painful adjustments. The water that starts out from the furthest reaches of the world flows secretly, one wave at a time. The bay doesn't understand the changes the water will bring to it and it awakens one day, different. Like the bay, I didn't wonder about my new status as a fatherless child. But out of respect and affection, I went on calling him Papa.

I transferred the admiration I'd had for my father onto Mr. Lafontaine who took all my questions seriously, even the most foolish ones, and who offered new intellectual challenges that demanded days and days of reflection.

"Tremblay, I want you to consider the following problem: for a citizen, what is the relationship between rights and individual responsibility?"

Returning home, I ran up to my room and attacked the issue methodically. Three sheets of paper. On the left the rights, in the centre the citizen, on the right the responsibilities.

My father came in. He had invited a couple friends over, along with their daughter who was my age, and they were waiting for me in the yard.

I pulled myself away from my three sheets of white paper, though I carried the three words inside me out into the yard. Once we were introduced to each other, my father told me that Marilyne loved travelling and discovering new places, and Marilyne, who wasn't shy at all, reeled off the journeys she had made with her parents to 'exotic' countries. "Haiti is fabulous, it's like they cut down the trees on the mountains to make them more beautiful." In a sombre voice, I described the erosion caused by deforestation, itself the result of poverty. Marilyne said, "Ah, so you know the place. Maybe they're poor, but I certainly didn't see any poor people, they all looked so happy." I said nothing and she pushed on. From one Club Med to the next, she had visited Senegal, Mexico, and Tunisia, and had returned with all the clichés imaginable about Blacks, Latinos, and Arabs. I listened but didn't try to put her in her place. She blurted out the stereotypes in such a pretty voice, stopping to smile and lean in my direction, to tell me some petty secret and let me glimpse the top of her breasts. I forgot all about words and my passion for debate. That was when I understood that learning to live with girls was not going to be easy. That night, I masturbated with dreams of Marilyne. I had all the trouble in the world falling asleep.

That desire, for it *was* desire, would never lead to love, I was sure of it. But there was no use denying it, desire did exist, and as I studied my three sheets of paper and the three words on them the next morning, I could think only about her breasts and how much I wanted to see them. Was that the animal in the human pushing to the surface? Love, desire, animality, and most of all sex, *terra incognita*, all these things foreign to me, I couldn't learn about the world and master these mysterious currents of the soul at the same time, neurons and, as they said about sex, the perfumes and language of the body. I wanted to change the world and had so little time to try and decipher the mysteries, rustlings, stolen smiles, and

missed looks. The road seemed to stretch out before me:
I would learn about life through life.

But for the time being, as they said about the mystics,
I had to mortify my flesh to wipe away the thought of
Marilyne's breasts and finish my work on rights, responsibilities, and the citizen. I concluded by explaining that
rights could not be asserted at the expense of duties and
that the citizen had to first think of the common good.

Mr. Lafontaine told me he was running a small group
dedicated to reflecting on issues and political action. At
times the group participated in demonstrations with
unions and community organizations. If I wanted to
attend a meeting, he would be glad to welcome me. I was
familiar with worldwide injustice, violent racism, dicta-
torship, and civil wars, but I knew very little, except via
the television, about poverty in my own city. On that first
meeting, the floor dropped out from underneath my
feet – several times.

On that fine early autumn day, I showed up at Mr.
Lafontaine's house in Pointe-Saint-Charles. Small, red-
brick houses with crumbling facades that gave directly
onto the sidewalk, televisions bellowing out the open
windows, children in raggedy clothes playing in the
street, and old people, lots and lots of old men out
walking with no particular destination. Shouting, noise,
dirt, and unfamiliar odours, rusty cars, fat women sitting
in front of their houses. I'd seen slums before, but not
entire streets of slums; I'd seen poor people too, but not
a neighbourhood made up entirely of them. I was
discovering that injustice existed in my country. It wasn't
the same poverty, but it was poverty all the same. These
weren't foul-smelling shacks where entire families were
thrown together, but they were slums, and none too
pleasant, that held large families. No one was dying of
hunger like in Ethiopia, but these were people from
Quebec who had empty stomachs in one of the richest

societies in the world.

I walked slowly and sometimes lingered to look around. I didn't feel very comfortable. I wasn't observing, I was like a voyeur or a traveller in an exotic land. I took pictures with my mind's eye to be able to tell the tale afterward.

Mr. Lafontaine's house stood out from the others. The façade had been redone and the bricks were a bright red colour that I later learned was called vermillion. It had windows with dark wood frames, all decorated with planters overflowing with geraniums and pansies. A young vine was beginning to climb the bricks.

"I came here to live with real people," Mr. Lafontaine said, taking in the whole neighbourhood.

He was wearing sandals instead of the leather shoes he usually wore, and washed-out blue jeans and a black t-shirt with red letters that spelled out "Neither Law nor Order."

"Come in."

His casual manner surprised me. The house itself was a library. Walls of books, piles of them in the hallway, and on the kitchen table. It was also a shrine. Picasso reproductions, a picture of Karl Marx, Rosa Luxemburg, a poster of the Bonnot gang, the celebrated photo of Che Guevara, and one of Castro.

"We're going to discuss the demonstration we plan to participate in next November."

A dozen people or more, all wearing the same t-shirt, had gathered in the dining room. Mr. Lafontaine said my name, and the discussion resumed. I quickly understood that these people infiltrated demonstrations staged by pressure groups and community organizations and, through provocation, tried to push the authorities, especially the police, into acts of repression. They talked about State oppression, the Nazi police, wage slavery, and class struggle. The language seemed a little exaggerated to my taste and, in my timid fashion, I put forward some quiet reservations. They looked at me as if I were part of the Nazi police force. "He's young, he's evolving, but I think Claude will come to see that the ends justify the means when the cause is right." Then Maria exploded.

"In Chile, my mother is turning over in her grave and howling with pain." Her heavy Spanish accent turned her words into a melodramatic tirade that had something comic about it, but I held back my laughter. "My mother was raped and tortured, disappeared, and thrown into a hole somewhere, never to rest. I will fight, I will claw their eyes out, I want the oppressor's blood." I was looking for the oppressor here, in my own city. It was capitalism, perhaps, but it didn't dig holes for all the mothers of all the Marias. Her arms snaked like a tango dancer, and her eyes were aflame. "Chile and Quebec, it's the same struggle," Maria declared. She was beautiful.

One part of me, the part I didn't care for since it escaped my control, figured that if I knew her better, I'd understand her point of view. For a logical, solid person such as myself, discovering that a woman's eyes could challenge all the certainties I had so slowly and methodically acquired created a kind of fear. But I decided that life would teach me about women. Faithful to my method, I let life take over.

I listened to Maria's proposal for action. It made me curious: the Montreal Chamber of Commerce was organizing a gourmet buffet at the Queen Elizabeth Hotel for two hundred dollars a plate; the benefits would go to food banks and soup kitchens. The beneficiaries of this corporate largesse had decided to protest, maintaining that they received only a pittance of the sums raised. Maria proposed that we carry out a raid and make off with the plates of foie gras, quail, filet mignon, and salmon *en papillote*, and distribute it symbolically to the groups demonstrating in front of the hotel. My rational mind noted the problems in her plan. The first one was moral. We would be usurping the cause and the reputation of organizations that were making great efforts to deliver meals and provisions to people who had neither. I thought we'd risk undermining the credibility of the groups and their militants who had chosen non-violent political action to advance their cause. We would end up stealing the spotlight. But this time, I kept quiet. People would forget the real activists, former welfare recipients and community organizers who had created small spaces of relative abundance, volunteers, good-hearted individuals, basically. We risked getting in their way, as our interpretation of necessary radical action overran their resolute, patient approach, often their lives' work. Maria's passion, her elegant fury, swept aside all moral qualms like a hot wind scattering forgotten leaves on an otherwise perfectly raked lawn.

When she pushed aside her hair that cascaded across her face, the movement of her arm was graceful beyond words. My technical hesitations about what tactics to employ to gain entry to the hall, in a group and by force, or individually and discreetly, about how to carry the food, considering how heavily loaded down we would be while attempting to escape, and then how to transfer the fruit of our revolutionary larceny to the food banks, all the questions I didn't ask melted away before a single one of her ballerina moves.

The group was carried away with its own enthusiasm. We congratulated ourselves. Maria smiled; maybe she was thinking of her mother in the grave. A person can smile and still be sad. Wanting to share my enthusiasm, I declared that we would be contemporary Robin Hoods who stole from the rich to give to the poor. If looks could kill, Maria would have done just that.

Mr. Lafontaine saved me by pointing out that Robin Hood and Arsène Lupin and the Bonnot Gang were simply ways of referring to complex revolutionary work. Maria stopped staring daggers at me.

We don't just decide we're adults, it happens by itself, it comes to us whether we know it or not, and it's only much later that we might confide in a friend, or a woman we are courting, "That's when I finally grew up."

Walking toward the subway, awash in my new revolutionary audacity, convinced I was going to participate in an important moment in the awareness-building of the people, at age seventeen I told myself that I finally had a goal: to build a better world for the children of tomorrow. They wouldn't have to play out in the street. The slums would recover their dignity and become solid workers' housing.

"Father, I'm going to participate in my first demonstration. We're going to…"

"Demonstrations are for assholes. They're for losers and dreamers."

"You're exaggerating. Don't tell me you never demonstrated when you were young."

"Of course I demonstrated. It was a waste of time. You can't change anything. It's too late. Anyway, you're too young to understand."

I felt his contempt, a primal and instinctive rejection of the hope that my words expressed. He criticized me because I was playing less tennis. He drank his whisky in small sips, but he could have just as well drunk off half the glass in one swallow. His little sips followed each other at a quick and regular pace, like a machine equipped with a program that organized the methodical and systematic absorption of liquid. Since when had his face become greyer than his hair? And his shoulders so slumped, and the crow's feet so sudden as if they had come to wipe away his features during my short absence? Why hadn't I seen that my father was wasting away and drinking more and more?

My father was in bad shape. The adult I had become saw that, but the child I remained, too disturbed by the change, retreated to his room without asking any questions, and without daring to go further, as if I were an adult outside the house or in my room, but never when I stood before my parents. Especially where my father was concerned. His abrupt changes of mood, his cynicism, and his ready-made answers left me in a state of confusion, since I must have thought his behaviour was a façade that concealed some fearful disorder or secret despair. At seventeen, you don't ask your father why he's so nasty to you, why he's drinking so much, and why his face is greyer than his hair. My father belonged to a part of life I could not bring myself to analyse or even accept. I realized that I understood nothing, and sought refuge in the outside world that was becoming ever clearer to me. Life would make it its business to reveal its mysteries to me. For the time being, I had my books and the paper about poverty in Montreal that Mr. Lafontaine assigned me. Debate excited me. Poverty was not absolute; it was relative and proportionate to the neighbouring wealth. Even if the poor person in my country was a hundred times richer than the poor person in Rwanda, in his flesh and in his mind he is as poor as his African counterpart, and so the merry-go-round turned. I talk about the merry-go-round now, because since then, I've met poor Africans who dreamed of becoming poor Canadians, but never the other way around. I understood that the poor people in Mr. Lafontaine's area were much more numerous than I'd thought. That strengthened my resolve to take action. That, and Maria's coal-black eyes.

5

It was no kind of weather for the poor and ill-clothed to be outside, yet fifty or so of them were out there in the November snow-shower, half rain and half snow, heavy wet flakes sticking to their coats and faces. The humid wind blew right through them. They were the group we were infiltrating, and they were chanting polite slogans that we repeated along with them, "No *foie gras*, give us hamburger meat!" "A banquet for the rich, nothing for the poor!" It was a symbolic protest whose only goal was thirty seconds on TV after the minute about the charitable work of the *foie gras* eaters.

There were twenty of us, and we knew the drill. No one knew anyone else, we weren't carrying placards, and we were positioned at equal intervals in the line of militants parading in front of the doors of the Queen Elizabeth Hotel as four benevolent policemen looked on, as frozen as the protesters. When Mr. Lafontaine and Jorge, another Chilean refugee, dashed into the hotel, two policemen ran after them, and Katarina, a young pregnant woman, fainted in front of a policeman who turned to his colleague for help. Mr. Lafontaine and Jorge headed left, toward the moving stairway that led down to the train station. They had a train to catch, they explained to the policemen. A dozen of us surged into the hotel. One floor up, and we were in the large banquet hall. Maria was next to me. We were supposed to grab several plates of food, hand them over to the representatives of the poor, and then fade into the snowy streetscape like urban Robin Hoods. But the guests took exception to our action. They tried to block us, some of them even used their fists to save their dearly bought food from our raid. Maria grabbed a large platter and I picked up two lobsters. The stairway again, the exit onto Mansfield, people staring at us, we turned right onto René-Lévesque to catch up to the demonstrators. With my two lobsters, I attracted all the attention. But there was no one. The poor people and their representatives had disappeared. But Maria was a real member of the resistance; she was never caught off guard.

"Get in the cab, Claude," she said, and jumped into the nearest taxi. I followed her with my two lobsters. Not a word in the cab; from the rear-view mirror, the driver's suspicious eyes watched the platter and the two crustaceans. I kept looking out the back window, convinced the police were chasing us.

Her apartment on Park Avenue above a Greek bar was tiny. On the living-room walls was a photo of Allende, and another of Che, the famous one. Piles of books stood on the floor. A Cuban flag separated the living room from the kitchen.

Maria set the platter on the table. "What's that stuff?" I told her it was pâté. Dark pink slices, marbled with brown and chestnut, surrounded by golden jelly. "You should never waste food," Maria said. She came back from the kitchen with two plates and silverware. "It was sort of fun," I commented. Maria told me that the revolution must never be fun. We ate our lobsters in silence. I wasn't having any fun. I was thinking of how our operation had failed. It was a humiliating defeat: two lobsters and some pâté eaten by two revolutionaries.

I searched for the right words to politely announce my departure, without mentioning our failure.

"Do you want to make love?" She could have been asking me if I wanted a cup of coffee. I knew about coffee, but I didn't know about love. She got up and cleared the table. I heard her set down the plates and throw away the pâté behind the Cuban flag. Looking creates desire and from desire springs love. "Well?" In theory, I knew that, as she stood there before me in front of the Cuban flag, her hands on her hips, I should have felt the stirring of an erection. Desire, even. Then I remembered my method.

"I'd like to look," I said shyly, and launched into a long explanation about the gaze, and desire, and love, but I couldn't get the words into the right sequence, and I stammered a series of broken phrases. She took off her t-shirt, then her bra. She wasn't smiling. She stood in front of the Cuban flag like a revolutionary statue. She didn't even look at me. "Now what?" I had no answer. Desire is not born from an admiring glance. I had never seen such pretty breasts, but I hadn't seen any breasts at all outside of reproductions in dictionaries. I didn't even have the urge to touch her. She slid down her jeans and spread her legs. She was completely naked, and for the first time I saw a woman's sex. Her eyes were distant. "Now that you've seen, you can touch." No. That wasn't how I wanted to begin my love life. I had to leave. I drank a beer in the dirty, moth-eaten Greek bar downstairs. Old men with sagging stomachs, dressed in clothes from another time, were playing video poker.

I would never understand anything about women. I had to tell her I was sorry. I rang at her door. Maria accepted my awkward, labyrinthine explanations, then told me how it worked as she paced the room, smoking a stinking cigar. Desire can only be sexual, with no attachments. Desire through love was invented by bourgeois literature, and it weakens revolutionary convictions. Militants must accept their quotient of animal feelings and satisfy their sexual impulses in an objective manner that does not contravene the struggle. She kneeled in front of me and unbuckled my belt. I was trembling as she pulled down my jeans and my underwear, and I didn't know what she was doing. She took my penis in her mouth. I thought erections were born of desire, but that turned out not to be true. She stood up, climbed onto the sofa, and straddled me. Then she went to work, her head thrown back, her eyes on the ceiling. I was just a tool in her personal quest.

It wasn't till after I came that I felt desire. I wanted to kiss her. She pushed me away.

As I went down the stairs, I wondered if she'd do the same thing with someone else tomorrow. I was jealous already, and I wanted to see Maria again. And not for the revolution, but for her, though she neither looked at me nor kissed me; she satisfied herself and returned me to my ignorant status, after teaching me about that curious pain called sexual pleasure.

The relative nature of poverty took up all my time. Maria was working on affordable housing and suggested we infiltrate FRAPRU, a community organization that was greatly respected, even if its recommendations were rarely followed. In spite of learning the building code by heart, the vacancy rate for rental properties, the Rent Board regulations, the list of delinquent slum-owners, and maintaining a registry, Maria paid no attention to my comments or my discoveries during our meetings. But my efforts did earn the admiring approval of Mr. Lafontaine, who pointed out that revolutionary passion must be based on hard-headed analysis of the objective conditions. I didn't try to get closer to Maria. I waited for the same thing to happen again. If she felt like repeating the experience, she would give me a sign and climb on top of me again.

"Father, is man an animal?"

"Yes."

"In all ways?"

"No. He has awareness."

"Can he only react like an animal in some ways, like for sex?"

"Of course."

"And change the way he behaves as a human to satisfy his animal nature?"

"Of course."

"And modify his objectives?"

"Yes."

"How can we be animals without betraying our conscience? I mean, and still stay human?"

Father poured himself a whiskey and swallowed it down. And then another one. Was that a tear, a sign of emotion? Mist settled over my father's eyes like a veil. I said I was sorry for bothering him. He stammered out an answer, it was all right, he was just tired. I went up to my room before he started crying, because I was old enough to know that after the mist comes rain.

My longing for Maria to take me back upset all my points of reference and logical analyses, and the care I took in planning an action. Because she was a refugee and the orphan girl of a woman who'd disappeared into a hole, she had a disproportionate influence over the group. She came up with a slogan for every situation, a scathing remark for every reasonable objection. She would talk fast, throw her hair back, cast withering glances, and mock the careful and the timid. I'm sure I wasn't the only one who thought Maria was leading us toward the dead-end of anarchy and pure provocation. But who were we, well-off members of the petty bourgeois, to contest the voice of the revolution incarnate? Had any of us ever suffered? She had, in her flesh and her memory. Her rage and passion made us seem small and cast us back onto our comfortable existences and our fear of risk. The Queen Elizabeth Hotel operation had been an enormous disaster, but no one questioned the basic rightness of the undertaking. By exploiting the shame we felt at not having a mother in a hole somewhere, Maria convinced us. As far as I was concerned, all she had to do was move and I lost all critical faculties.

6

My mother asked me why I was now more interested in local news and less in international events. That was an excuse to talk; she followed this by asking me what I thought about my father's mood. She didn't mention his grey face, or the whiskey, or his silence, or the distance he created between us, as if he weren't living with us anymore, but next to us, on a path parallel to ours, on the same street, but moving along the opposite sidewalk.

I replied that poverty begins at home, and to change the world, justice first had to come to our own country.

"What does your father think?"

"He won't talk about it. He says it's normal, that's just the way the world works, and we can't do anything about it."

"Did you know that your father, before he entered the civil service…No, that doesn't matter. I think he's tired. You're right, we have to change things here, but you shouldn't forget people who are objectively a lot worse off and exploited than we are."

Mother was a communications consultant, and press secretary to Robert Charlebois. She was invited to all the openings, she shopped at Holt Renfrew and Roche-Bobois, but used words like 'objectively' and 'exploited'. That must have been a mistake, a kind of slip due to the popularity of certain terms that become part of the landscape without anyone thinking about what they really mean.

7

At college, I wasn't the first in anything anymore. I got thrown off the hockey team and lost my tennis games on a regular basis. Since I started wearing the beginnings of a beard and letting my hair grow, the girls chased after me. I felt only indifference. I didn't have a lot of friends left, since I spent most of the time criticizing them for not wanting to change the world. I speechified and issued proclamations. I didn't listen to anyone. I talked like Maria whose mother was at the bottom of a hole, except that my mother was accompanying Robert Charlebois to a TV show tonight. After a discussion about burning down the slums, I gave my phone number to Maria who balled up the sheet of paper where I'd also written some thoughts about methodology. Why not renovate the slums, and engage in construction instead of destruction? Maria never called. I learned to tame my animal nature through masturbation, but the feverish exercise left me with the bitter taste of guilt, as if I had been unfaithful to Maria. During our group meetings, she took up most of the space. Mr. Lafontaine generally kept quiet. New members were monopolising the debates. There were twenty of them or so, in jeans and sleeveless t-shirts, chains around their belts. They were into street-fighting. Society is shit. That was true, but you have to explain what the shit was, analyse it, and choose your objectives. That's what I thought, but kept my thoughts to myself. One day, I was sure, I'd reconcile my logic and my needs, the facts and desire.

Maria stopped talking about the slums and started

issuing speeches about American imperialism, the cause of all injustice around the world, and the symbols we needed to destroy. I could say, "Let's begin with the slums." But she launched into a diatribe about McDonald's exploiting Latin American peasants and poisoning poor people here. I didn't say anything, and tried to catch her eye instead. Maria wanted to destroy a McDonald's. She was too busy to look at me, but the more her project took shape, the greater her passion grew, and her gestures and attitudes seduced me all the more. It was stupid to destroy a restaurant, and I understood that even veteran members of the group weren't hot on the idea, and Mr. Lafontaine had reservations about the use of violent action not based on large-scale popular discontent. A Latino spat, "Petty-bourgeois shit! People's consciousness is born from violent action!" My mentor went quiet, and I saw Maria agreeing.

The plan was simple: choose a relatively isolated McDonald's, smash the windows with a heavy hammer, throw a dozen Molotov cocktails in selected spots so the fire would spread, then run. Not a word about the alarm system that would go off after the first hammer blow, or how much time we had to do the job, or how to make our getaway. We set the place on fire and melt away into the night. Maria handed out instructions about how to put together a Molotov cocktail and advised us to make a few to practice. Mr. Lafontaine declared he was opposed to this slide into anarchy, and that as far as he was concerned, the group no longer existed. The meetings went on at Maria's place.

I remember my first attempt. I took an empty bottle of Côte de Beaune Village and filled it with barbecue lighter fluid. I didn't seal the bottle correctly. I threw it against a rock in the park, and was rewarded with a *poof!* sound and a weak trail of flame. I tried again the next day with a Johnny Walker Black Label bottle. The rock exploded and flames lit up the park. I ran like the devil and by the time I got to my house, a hundred metres away, the night was filled with sirens. My father asked me if I'd heard the explosion. I couldn't get to sleep that night; I vacillated between the exaltation that came from entering the world of action, and the strange and troubling feeling that I was a prisoner on a rollercoaster that forced the thrill of pleasure on me.

I was still an attentive student in Mr. Lafontaine's class. Without saying anything out loud, we agreed not to mention Maria. But there I was, involved, burning with hope, gnawed by doubt and fear, and he was responsible for that. As a way of acknowledging the role he played in my life, the day before the attack on the McDonald's on Bellechasse Street, I told him about the plan. "You're making a very big mistake, Tremblay, but sometimes you have to go the wrong way to learn what you need to learn."

8

At the house, I had my choice of empty bottles. For my baptism by fire, I chose a Vosne-Romanée whose praises my father had sung through the entire meal the previous evening, and later on as well, as he sipped an old Armagnac that led him into drunkenness loaded with heavy sadness and vindictive commentary. I distrusted the effects of alcohol but accepted the inebriation of action, as if the latter was nobler and less destructive.

Becoming a man takes time, and you need more than the right age to reach adulthood. When it came to theoretical knowledge of the world, with its power relations and perverse complexities, I had almost reached my goal. But in real life, I sailed chaotically on a naïve adolescent sea. I knew nothing of the currents and storms, and I tacked this way and that, ignorant and open to every influence that might affect my destination. I let the waters carry me along.

When it came to action, I remembered how my legs had failed me in the stairway of the Queen Elizabeth Hotel as if I had never been a top-level athlete. Stealing two lobsters had paralysed my reflexes and I had to stagger down the stairs.

Maria entrusted her Latinos with the first wave of the attack – breaking the three plate-glass windows – and gave the hard-boiled anarchists the job of throwing the incendiary bombs. I was part of the third wave with several members of the group.

The objective was well chosen. The McDonald's stood by a big park, alongside commercial properties, on a street travelled by few drivers at night. The Latinos attacked with revolutionary fervour, and the windows burst into a thousand pieces. The first Molotov cocktail set off a wave of applause. Shit, this wasn't a show. Then, magically, the restaurant lit up from the inside. Thirty or so policemen equipped with bulletproof vests and armed with automatic weapons surged out of the shadows. They were waiting for us, they had allowed us to break the windows to prove the offence, then throw one Molotov cocktail so we could be accused of arson. Caught in the act, an open and shut case for the prosecution.

I don't know why, but when a policeman slapped on the handcuffs and told me I had the right to remain silent and that anything I might say could be used against me, I felt free. A heavy burden had been lifted from me. Maria was screaming, pouring out her anti-imperialist venom and kicking the policemen. She was ridiculous, and my complicity in this nonsensical operation brought me back to reality. It was time for me to return to myself.

In youth court, I pleaded guilty and was sentenced to three months in a detention centre. I had three months to think about my future. As I contemplated the non violent ways of changing the world in a little room, three metres by five metres, my father committed suicide.

He scribbled a few last words, probably for himself: "Why live if you don't do anything after you've dreamed of doing everything?"

I had attacked a restaurant and killed my father. I felt responsible, but not guilty.

Did I really love Maria? No, surely not, since not a single cell in my body reacted when I learned she had been deported to Chile.

9

Four to one for Holland. People fight loneliness by building approximations of happiness from whatever is at hand. To fight loneliness, they imagine future pleasures. A dinner, a walk, a soccer game with a team they can identify with, or a duck they think they can recognize in the park on the way to the Court, or the plan to buy a gift for someone. I had entrusted my evening's happiness in a victory for France. Bunia was cancelled, and France humiliated. I am thinking of my mother, and the evening I returned after three months' detention in a centre for young offenders, and my father's suicide.

10

My parents met at a lecture by René Dumont, the French agronomist who wrote *False Start in Africa*. My father, Julien, was studying philosophy, but he dreamed of a career on stage as well, and also considered working in Africa. At the same time, he wondered if law wouldn't be more suitable, or maybe even the priesthood, but in a workers' church. His idealism, his naivety, and his generosity were charming; so was his timidity. My mother, Rosanne, was leading the revolution in Brittany-style *crêperies*, and sometimes joined the demonstrations according to her latest encounter. She went from Marxist-Leninist to Trotskyist to Maoist to anarchist, according to the latest flavour. My father called her his Rosa Luxemburg.

The revolution was divided into two camps: the rigorous Soviet, Chinese, or Algerian, take your pick, it was prudish and stark. Then there was the *revolución*, cigars, machos, and pasionarias. The Cuban model always won over the other side. Change the world by fucking and drinking rum.

The revolution kept my mother entertained. Father listened to her ready-made slogans and formulas and started reading everything she hadn't read but referred to constantly, Marx, Engels, Bakunin, Lenin, Trotsky, and Mao. Julien didn't become a communist to win her over, but my mother believed that without necessarily wanting to, she had led him to that path.

He abandoned philosophy for political science. In her mind, the revolution was a form of escape, of entertainment, inebriation. She stopped being the bourgeois daughter of a woman who owned Montreal's major arts production company. She was Rosa Luxemburg now.

Then came the proletarian period that my mother adored at first. Living with the exploited of Saint-Henri, discussions with the workers, the unemployed, people on welfare, the wretched of the earth. After his M.A., Julien left university and for a few months he dedicated himself to setting up a paper, the *Worker's Forum*. He became a hard-core Marxist-Leninist. She didn't understand anything of his speeches on building the avant-garde through infiltration. He began working at the Hôtel-Dieu hospital as a nurse's aide. At six o'clock every morning, with a handful of comrades, he passed out leaflets at factory gates. At the hospital, he set up a cell within the union and gave thirty percent of his pay to the Party. Their neighbours didn't eat the way they did, they spoke a completely different language than theirs, and they voted for the most reactionary parties. But Julien kept on. Mother fell out of love with the proletariat. After three years of revolutionary practice, dead-ends, and disillusionment, my father announced that capitalism had won because the workers had become consumers now. It was time to join the system and improve it from within. Julien became a bureaucrat with the Ministry of Education. Rosanne was pregnant with me. Her mother-in-law helped them buy a duplex on Waverly Street, just in time for me to be born into a proper environment. My mother rediscovered her true nature, like a snake with a new skin that is just a copy of the old one. With renewed pleasure, she went back to her soirées, bought herself an elegant new wardrobe, and began to cultivate her garden.

She died five years after he did in a car accident, dashing from one meeting to the next as she always did. My new status as an orphan didn't change my existence much.

I was too absorbed in my studies and my research to notice anyone around me. That was just before Nathalie came into my life.

11

I'd read a lot of books about incarceration, isolation, and torture. In the kind of novels I liked, isolation led to the light and torture, to the reappropriation of the body. In youth detention centres, torture doesn't exist and isolation is a relative thing. I might have been a political prisoner, but I was shooting pool with small-time delinquents and strong-arm guys who had neither words nor dreams. I should have gone after the cash register at McDonald's. Mario had 'done' three corner stores. Partly for his mother, but mostly to buy coke. Coke because life isn't fair, and when you're high, you forget that. You forget what? "That life isn't fair, fuck! How many times do I have to tell you?" Mario was cross-eyed, and you couldn't meet his gaze. He stalked the premises silently like a hyena trying to scavenge leftovers. He got along all right, running a business for nickels. "Life ain't fair, Claude." There are laws and lawyers and courts, Mario. "Not for us there aren't."

I didn't learn anything about myself in prison (and I did like the word "prison"), but I did learn about Mario, who was a petty criminal and, if God gave him enough time, would become a true criminal. "Claude, when I get out of here, I'm going to knock over a bank and buy my mother a house." His revenge against life would be understandable, and easy to explain, but would it be fair? It wouldn't be legal, but maybe it would be justified. The trainers talked to us about reintegration and accepting the rules of life. And what if reintegrating and observing the rules and the way life ran meant you had to accept injustice? Our isolation made us ask too many questions, and when it came to cross-eyed Mario, he cried every night – I knew that for a fact. Mario wasn't a bad sort, just one of those bottom dogs that needed help getting back on his feet.

He knocked over his bank and got ten years.

12

At twenty-four, I got married in church. That was what Nathalie's parents wanted. She stated her request timidly, all but saying she was sorry, since she wasn't a practicing Catholic. But she wanted a wedding with a white dress with a train and flower girls and a reception with bouquets on every table. For me, that meant a tuxedo, a best man or two, and a visit to the parish priest. Everyone would be pleased and no principles would be violated, except my own lack of belief, but in Quebec, the fact that you were an unbeliever never turned into a political or philosophical stance.

I was finishing my master's in international law, and we were both 'leftists.' I learned you had to choose what you needed from solitude. My church wedding was a pleasant distraction, along with moving into a new apartment and the inevitable visits to Ikea, and the choice of colours for the walls. I didn't invest much in the process, but I participated out of respect for Nathalie, who put a lot of stock in those things.

When my mother died, I inherited a certain amount of money, but I had never touched it. Nathalie got a job as a researcher for a Catholic NGO. Even before the name caught on, we were yuppies.

Sometimes a place can change us just as much as an event. Nathalie couldn't spend a day without paging through a French interior decorating magazine. She worried about the door handles I hadn't even noticed, and showed me ceramic tiles that, per square metre, cost more than the object they were meant to set off. Her feel for harmony, her ability to bring together colour and form, and choose the seemingly banal object that would magically reinvent a useless shelf and create a new space for the eye to explore – all that astonished me. She applied herself so seriously and so patiently to building the environment for her daily life that I couldn't help but follow along on her search for the ideal décor. Her need for physical harmony enchanted me.

During my stay at the youth detention centre, I chose the path that Mario rejected. I opted for the rule of law; the patient application of the law would lead the Marios of the future onto the straight and narrow, a Christian expression if there ever was one. I decided that passion gave birth only to excess and stupidity, that desire must yield before admiration and community of thought, that love between a man and a woman must be founded on mutual respect, and that physical attraction was a trap. I hadn't known it, but Nathalie had been looking for a husband. Not a man or a lover, just a husband. I did the trick, and so she was satisfied.

She would put down her design magazine with an irritated look when I started talking to her about impunity and international justice, the subject of my doctoral thesis. I was asking a simple yet unsolved question. Impunity, especially in Africa, prevented the establishment of a society based on law and organized around fairness. That was a grave problem given that these places were confronting crimes that went far beyond the offences that judges schooled in normal legal tradition had to face. Do we judge an isolated rape case the same way we would the systematic policy of mass rape? Do we display the same legal circumspection toward a massacre of 800,000 people and the settling of accounts in a biker gang? Law answered yes; justice told me no. The more I studied law, the more I wondered whether it wasn't the first enemy of justice.

Nathalie would answer with an ambiguous noise that

was neither yes nor no. We made no decisions; things just took care of themselves. We made love once a week in adequate fashion, seriously and a little systematically, respecting the rules of engagement and always finishing in the missionary position. I was absorbed by the court of Arusha that was judging the *génocidaires* of Rwanda with more respect for procedure than necessary. Nathalie was looking for new kitchen cupboards. We talked less and less. After two years of married life, I found out she had a lover. I hadn't kissed her in six months. For my Ph.D., I compiled entries concerning statements of rape victims in international trials. "Évangéline Murozowa, age seventeen, student in the social sciences, raped by eighteen militiamen at a checkpoint in Gitarama." The judges did not accept her testimony because Évangéline could not prove that the accused had actually participated in the rape since, in all honesty, she admitted that in the darkness, the faces above her all had the same mad glint in their eyes. She did not want to lie to the tribunal or risk perjuring herself because she believed in God and had brought her own Bible on which she would swear her oath. "The entire hill knew that Évariste decided everything that happened at that checkpoint, and that he was always there." Hearsay, the defence objected, and the judges granted it. Two hundred survivors said the same thing; were they all unreliable witnesses? Was the entire hill an unreliable witness? Was Évariste the first to rape her, or the seventh, or the last? Could she describe any distinguishing marks on his body? Did she see him afterward? Did he rape her again? If not, why had he done it only once? Did she believe that, by achieving official victim status, she would receive financial compensation and, by the way, hadn't she taken on substantial debts before the incident? I imagined

Évangéline's pain and incomprehension after having been raped eighteen times, and how she did not answer a single question, probably because she was sobbing and the defence lawyer used her tears as a springboard to make her feel even more fragile and retreat further into silence. Drying her tears, she admitted she had used the microcredit issued by an NGO to buy a sewing machine and start producing clothing for children. She was behind in her payments. The defence lawyer cut his cross-examination short once she confessed to her state of financial peril.

Of course, the accused had been at home the whole time, eating grilled goat with his wife and five children. The hill accused him because he was the mayor and the representative of the State, and Tutsis didn't like Hutus. Eichmann often dined at home as the trains pulled into Treblinka and Jews didn't like Nazis either, that was a well-established fact.

I told Nathalie the story of Évangéline in the hope, I think, of establishing the lines of communication again. A woman's story should affect another woman. I added more details to try and touch her emotions. Nathalie listened attentively, but did not seem moved by the story. She took a sip of wine and even before she spoke a word, I knew it was over, especially my search for feelings of comfort. I would never be happy, that's what she was about to tell me. "How can I get interested in your story? That might happen in Africa, but not here. There's nothing there that concerns me, and as for that poor girl, I can't do anything for her. It's sad, but there's us and there's them, and we don't live on the same planet. I'd like to help them, give them money or demonstrate, but we have important things to do here too."

I didn't ask what. Affordable housing, Christmas baskets, a dollar thrust into an open hand in the damp February cold. I didn't understand this 'us' and this 'them', as if rape that happened somewhere else wounded and shattered a person less than rape here.

I think the time I spent with encyclopaedias, dictionaries, and atlases when I was a boy, and later a student, removed the idea of 'us' and 'them', In those works and compilations, rape isn't relative, it just is, period. The poor don't have any particular colour, their poverty is what defines them in a common, universal way. In the Larousse, a woman is a woman. She isn't more or less a woman depending on her country of origin. I developed simple notions from books. All human beings are the same, they have the same rights, they are brothers and sisters together, each responsible for the other's happiness. Nathalie believed that if she were raped, it would be more tragic than Évangéline. There was no sense trying to reason with her. Her vagina was superior and more precious than an African woman's. We shared nothing, save for a few TV shows and the occasional nature documentary. She decorated; I cooked and cleaned house. We accommodated each other, which meant that, literally, we were a convenience for each another. I gave up on desire and love, not because I had stopped believing in those things, but because they were too demanding. Compiling files on the planet's victims and the great perpetrators satisfied my emotional needs. And it wasn't because I was without love that my heart was empty of feeling and affection. On the contrary. As for Nathalie, she found her passion in her own comfort, her immediate environment, her career, and her clothes. She had no energy for the demands love made. She took a lover who, she confided in me, complained she wasn't loving enough. We laughed – laughed at ourselves.

Nathalie refused to come into my office where the walls were covered with terrible images. A young girl from Mozambique holding a human head in her hands, another girl from Uganda whose breasts had been sliced off, and a boy from Angola, no older than twelve, smoking a joint with a Kalashnikov between his legs. I am neither perverse nor morbid. Like icons, the photos reminded me of my promise that, for the moment, was leading me nowhere, but I was experiencing it the way a seminarian does, learning, reflecting, praying before entering the service of the Lord and His flock. The pictures displayed images of saints of both sexes who encouraged my vocation. I would do something.... But what? I didn't know. As I finished my thesis, I surfed the sites of international organizations and NGOs, but the jobs that interested me required on-the-ground experience I didn't have, and besides, the ground frightened me.

One day, Nathalie disappeared from my life. I can put it that simply because, for her, it was a day like any other, like any other of her mornings I knew. She spent a half hour putting on makeup, measured out her cup of Müslix, read a French magazine, and agreed to meet me for lunch at the *Deux Singes* on Saint Viateur Street. She kissed me on the forehead and wished me luck with my thesis defence. When I returned, a note was waiting on the living-room table. "You're always thinking about people who are suffering in the world. But really you're only thinking of yourself. Goodbye." The closets were empty.

13

Is there any place on this earth quieter and calmer than that pebbly shore in Brittany where I sought refuge after the failure of my marriage? The stones were warm. The sea had deserted the Bay of Paimpol. Only a few small pools amid the oyster beds recalled its presence. Silence does not exist, but the rustling leaves and the cries of the gulls create a kind of silence. Maybe silence is the peace of the earth, the sound it produces when it is at rest. A young woman was playing with a little girl as I watched the water advance like a lazy cloud across the sky. I weighed the pros and cons of reflection and action; in the reddening horizon I sought the path I would take. The woman and the girl greeted me as they went past. They were from Quebec, no mistaking that accent. The young woman's smile was so generous and warm. I immediately fell in love, but I answered no more than politely, nodding my head. Later the woman was drinking a Ricard and the girl was eating an ice cream in front of the Hôtel Bellevue. We nodded to one another and I decided their names were Isabelle and Emma. I don't know how else to express a woman's beauty other than by the turmoil she creates. I thought of all my mistakes, my inability to live with mystery, and I was afraid, afraid to try and say I was in love. At that very instant, I know now, I rejected the world's beauty and accepted the monotony of order and rules.

14

When do you really discover Africa? In the airplane, perhaps, between Paris and Abidjan. The women have put on their dashikis, the men show off their gold watches. The Whites seem more relaxed than on a Paris to London flight, even the ones wearing a tie. Or does it happen at the Abidjan airport? In the shoving and disorder, with the customs man who wants to confiscate your computer. The customs man never chooses the White traveller with experience. He chooses the neophyte going to Club Med, maybe, or the naïve one full of fine dreams and hopes, like the Black who shows up at French customs, the land of equality and fraternity. The illusions are reciprocal.

African hospitality, like European fraternity, has to be negotiated. So far, the Africa you are discovering is just a European copy, even if it throws you off because it's the opposite of what you know. Here, they are trying to cheat the White man. In Europe, they are trying to imprison the Black.

Once you get past customs, then you're really in Africa. A hundred arms, a hundred legs, a hundred mouths come at the visitor. Promises of speed, comfortable taxis, I'll be your guide, boss. I hear the words and I'm fascinated by the light and shadow. The light is steady and the shadows move through it. No-one was waiting for me, so a thousand people were. Water, melon, banana vendors, baggage carriers, and taxi drivers who often didn't have a taxi. When you know nothing about Africa, it's the luck of the draw. The customs man informed me that AIDS didn't exist in Ivory Coast, and for ten dollars we agreed that maybe there were a few cases. My luck of the draw was named Youssef.

"You know, boss, I could cheat you because I can tell it's your first time in Africa. But then I say to myself that if I am honest, you will keep me. So maybe I'll just cheat you a little."

He burst out laughing, a laugh so good-hearted and convincing that I trusted him immediately.

In the taxi that wasn't a taxi, and that cost closer to Youssef's price than the one indicated in the foreign aid worker's manual, I thanked Nathalie. Though she didn't know it, and would not have wanted to, she helped bring me here. She respected my distance, my obsession, and never questioned them.

Youssef explained it all as he drove his car like in a video game littered with obstacles: pedestrians, goats, other cars swerving this way and that, mini-buses out of control. Turn signals didn't exist here, and neither did lights. The lampposts had nothing to contribute. Sometimes one gave off watery light. The warm wind wrapped around me like a cover. I imagined I was bathing in amniotic fluid, and drawing nourishment from it. I was in the warm, moist belly of Africa. Youssef's running commentary, the car horns, the figures moving past, the cooking fires, all these ghosts trudging through the darkness, this overabundance of life and noise made my head spin. When we reached the Hotel Tiama on the Plateau, Youssef asked me for more than the price we agreed on, but quickly explained why. The traffic was thicker than usual. The White man who has a favourable prejudice toward Africa is very slow to learn to say no. He knows he is relatively rich and the small act of thievery directed against him, and that he is aware of, irritates him, but at the beginning he prefers to cooperate in his own robbery as a sign of his empathy. It is, I admit, a very small example of impunity but, I would discover later, it is part of the culture and daily life and the survival reflex. It is a way of life, and the example comes from higher up. Could anyone ever set down rules and standards? How could you explain that the smallest theft, like the largest, must be punished?

The restaurant at the Hotel Tiama was Chinese, and so was the singer, and the few girls sipping on coloured water at the bar. Chinese rock is to rock what military music is to music. I had certainly seen prostitutes before, fleetingly in downtown Montreal, but never this close, never in the flesh, right in front of me. Three of them were placidly sucking on their straws, casting bored looks at the dining room that was all but empty. I couldn't help looking, examining them, noting their moves and expressions. Yes, they were beautiful, but their beauty wasn't what attracted me, and neither did their bodies. I was fascinated by their status as prostitutes, their trade, and how they accepted exploitation. I'm against stealing, but I accept being stolen from a little. I agree with legalized prostitution, even if the business disgusts me. Nathalie would say, "If you want to understand, try it out."

"Do you want to talk? You look sad." Yes, I want to talk, but I'm not sad, I'm curious. She didn't wait for my answer. She ordered a whisky for me and one for herself. My name is Claude, I'm Canadian, and I work in humanitarian aid. That's a nice job. My name is Lolita and I'm studying business, but life is hard for girl students. School costs so much. She answered my question before I could ask it. I understood her problem because I happened to know that since the International Monetary Fund started scrutinizing Ivory Coast, and more or less put the country under its tutelage, university tuition had skyrocketed. Maybe she wasn't a real prostitute, just another victim of global injustice forced to sell her body to escape her precarious existence.

"Doesn't it bother you, selling your body to strangers?"

"No. I only go with men I could get engaged to. They give me presents. It would be better to talk in your room."

Her name was Lolita and her parents lived in the Beijing suburbs. I wasn't going to believe that was her real name. I sat in the armchair, and she paced back and forth, answering my pushy questions.

"Lolita isn't your real name?"

She stopped in front of me and pouted.

"You think I'm a liar, you don't respect me because you're White and rich. If I'm not good enough for you, tell me now and I'll go."

I protested. I love her eyes and her slim waist and her legs. You want to see my legs? She dropped her skirt. Do you like? She quit pouting and put on a teasing look. Yes, I like, very beautiful.

"You are too shy, I like shy men, you need to relax."

I felt no desire, and wondered how I got myself into this mess. I didn't want to fuck a prostitute, but she was already completely naked and on her knees in front of me, unfastening my belt, pulling down my zipper.

"I will make you happy."

I didn't push her away. How do you explain to a beautiful woman, even if she's a prostitute, that, no, you aren't looking for pleasure, but only comprehension, explanation, meaning?

I was getting sucked off for free by a prostitute. That's not fair, I thought, I'm exploiting her, I'm using her. Once the job was done, Lolita got back into her clothes quickly. She ran one hand through her hair and put out the other one.

"A little present?"

I gave her twenty euros.

"You are all the same, you White men, you exploit us."

I certainly didn't want to exploit a woman's body, even if the woman was a liar. The normal present, I learned, varied between fifty and a hundred euros, depending on the generosity of the donor. I split the difference, seventy-five euros. Lolita left with the promise she'd visit again. Sleep did not come easily. I moved back and forth between the memory of pleasure and shame. Did you have to play unfair to get a place in the sun? What would have been a productive compromise, and what compromise would have forced me into further compromises? Did I have to accept getting ripped off to help the people who were ripping me off? I'd been in Africa twelve hours, and I wanted to leave already.

The next morning at breakfast, Lolita was eating with a loud-mouthed German who, it was obvious, was a better sugar daddy than me. She was holding his hand and amusing herself by preparing and giving him little forkfuls of food.

15

Catherine had been working for four years at the centre for the fight against AIDS in Treichville, in cramped, messy quarters at the end of an ill-smelling corridor that ran through the hospital's internal medicine ward. Cholera on the left, AIDS on the right. Her angular face was burned by the sun, but she'd acquired her colour in the street, not at the pool. Catherine was as thin as a stick, and dressed in a washed-out dashiki as if she wanted to advertise poverty that was not hers, or perhaps an independent spirit that could cause her problems in a job that involved a lot of representation. That was why I wore a dark jacket and a tie. Clothes amount to codes, of course, but they are also part of your toolbox. Are clothes a kind of compromise like the one I engaged in the night before? Catherine wasted no time telling me that she had been against my hiring as the officer in charge of legal affairs with the local authorities, but since I was there...

"Listen, Claude, there's no standing on ceremony here, except with the employees, the help, and the security guards. They want you to keep your distance. They like it that way. So far, we've gotten along very well without legal counsel, we make our arrangements, we palaver for hours on end, we offer them gifts – that's all in the budget. I throw dinners at my place and set out open bottles of whisky. The problem isn't that there aren't any laws – there are too many. Since the president decides everything, the members of Parliament propose all sorts of laws on unimportant things, the directors write up rules, and the bureaucrats who do no work ask

their staff to create forms that correspond to the new
rules that spring from the new laws. Every form and
every law, as innocent as it may look, exists for a reason.
It represents one more obstacle, a hoop to jump through
to get to the next office, and finally to the boss of all the
offices who might just accept to sidestep some ridiculous
law or overly bureaucratic rule. The boss can be the
minister, or the prime minister, or the president. Up
until now, we've been honing our craft. We've been
getting along all right."

Catherine's eyes were dark and feverish, dark, sad
circles on a woman who was only thirty-five or so. She
seemed to be carrying all the world's exhaustion on her
shoulders. Her emaciated features made me think of
Lolita, who was so happy this morning. Lolita,
Catherine, Youssef – Africa was doing nothing for me.
But Catherine did have an effect. "Come to the house
tonight, I've got a good cook and a wine cellar." Lonely
women recognize the signs of emotion in a man the way
migratory birds return periodically to the same cornfield
for food so they can continue their exhausting flight to
the next continent.

I love making people happy. Since I can't seem to
charm or impassion them, I have only good manners
and kindness to maintain harmonious relations with
them. Catherine was an unhappy woman. Her only
motivation was her project. The fish was overcooked.
Taking large mouthfuls of wine, she explained Africa to
me all over again. Everything she said terrified me.
Nothing works, everyone's corrupt, but get used to it.
You have to integrate, slip into the culture, and respect
it. Very quickly we were in bed and I did my duty to
provide pleasure, which was not unpleasant in itself. She
cooed like a dove, or maybe a pigeon, I'm not sure.
"Have you come to apply the funders' rules?" she asked.

"Yes. I'm going to apply the rules. Five thousand

doses of tritherapy each worth twenty thousand dollars a year, that's not a cheap gift. I have no intention of seeing a single dose end up on the black market or given to a sick bureaucrat as a present."

"Screw you, you poor, pretentious little White man. You want your aid to change everything!"

Of course I did. I was threatening Catherine's idea of Africa. Her Africa didn't need my clean conscience and my rules of good governance. I never understood why people mix everything up. They like to talk about cooking. I know that cooking reproduces the models of agricultural exploitation, the prices on world markets, shortages, and the histories of products. But cooking as a subject of conversation is good enough in itself, it can turn into poetry and evoke memories and places and events. We had just finished filling our mutual emptiness, and right away she started in telling me about good governance. I'd rather she tell me it wasn't great, and couldn't we start again, I would have made an effort, and concentrated on my erection, but no, dammit – good governance! Give me Lolita who ripped me off and cheated on me with anything on two legs, but at least she wouldn't talk to me about China and Tibetan independence. I was the prisoner of this mongoose woman who had dragged her sadness to the Dark Continent. Nothing could throw me off balance except for women. Catherine made me sad, she was killing me, but I stayed close to her slim body, I stroked her ribs with my fingertips. How could I leave in the middle of the night in Abidjan, leave this sad useless bed, a morose woman who, as a final indignity, pestered me about my mission that was under her supervision? I need to sleep, I said. I thought about the five thousand doses of tritherapy; I was responsible for their proper delivery and proper use by the Treichville hospital. Like in a nightmare, I listened to Catherine tell me that she liked me and hoped we would work together efficiently. Lolita, I miss your simple lies.

16

Catherine poured coffee and lectured me as if I were a child. She paced the kitchen, her breasts hanging, and declaiming all the while. A sight like that might be tolerable at night, when you're in bed, kissing, trading caresses, more or less in thrall to sexual error. That was how I thought of my adventures and encounters. When a woman exhibits the sadness of her body with no shame, either you love her or think you possess her. This is me and you'll love me as I am. By showing her body freely, Catherine was declaring her love – in the present, immediate, her African love, a thrust, an encounter, a smile that becomes a caress. There are no rules in a love like that, just the primal meeting between man and woman. Wanting is in control, need is too, as is desire. Catherine explained all that to me: the need to respect the rules even if they seem absurd. Don't be surprised by late arrival or errors. Say thank you when you want to slap someone, approve when you want to kill them, take it with a smile when they make their jokes about White people. Don't remind them that we're financing them and paying for their villas on the French Riviera. Shocked, I listened silently to the theory that guilty Whites must accept everything a Black person does. And if the Black man is a thief? Catherine's empty breasts say it's of no importance. Her driver took me to my meeting.

The elevator works one time out of two, the director of protocol explained. The gentleman sitting behind a wooden desk was just a pawn, and directed nothing at all, except two pretty girls. One was responsible for leading me to the elevator across from the protocol office, on which was written, "All Visitors Must Report to Protocol." She opened the door, pressed number 6, and closed the door. Nothing happened. The car turned into a cell because I couldn't open the door. I reasoned with myself. This is normal, predictable. We Westerners are too accustomed to technological efficiency, a sort of magic immediacy. We don't know what delays and waiting mean. After ten minutes in my cage, I knocked politely, hoping that a member of Protocol would hear and direct me to the stairway because I was now late for a very important meeting with the director of the Ministry of Health.

I knocked a little more insistently, and twenty minutes later, started yelling. The hostess opened the door and informed me that I was to press on the button twice. Why can't the door be opened from the inside? Why? She didn't know, and it was obvious she didn't understand why I didn't understand the protocol and why I had so many questions. I hit the 6 button twice. The elevator jerked upward as if it were suffering convulsions, and stopped at the fifth floor in a great rattling of chains. I used the stairway to make it to the sixth floor. Another director of protocol behind an empty desk. He asked me to sit down on a threadbare couch. I declined, and explained I was late because of the elevator. He didn't listen and began filling out a form, asking for my passport. He applied himself to his work, filling out a dozen lines of information, then informed me that due to my tardy arrival, I would have to wait until the director of the Ministry was free, or come back another day if it so happened that he had some more important mission. I waited two hours with my delivery order for five thousand doses of tritherapy, whose value was the equivalent of half the budget of Ivory Coast's Ministry of Health.

The director offered no explanation and no apologies for my having to wait two hours. He was the perfect fulfillment of every cliché, a parody of himself. He spoke in complete paragraphs, showed his predator's teeth, laughed at his own jokes, used the telephone as a prop, and kept glancing at his gold Rolex. He was setting a trap, but I didn't know which one it was. "You realize that the importation of medicines is strictly regulated." Yes, I knew that much. I had memorized all the laws relating to medicine. And there was a law that stipulated that all imported medicines must be submitted to the medical authorities. I'm not stupid, I checked everything, and the Authority has no laboratory. I imitated Catherine, but only up to a certain point. "We can give you a sample to be checked." That's when I learned that, scientifically, to correctly test the quality of a medication, a minimum of five hundred samples was required, a tenth of what Canada was willing to give! You're taking me for a fool, Maximilien. For that was his name: Maximilien. I pointed out that the number did not seem to correspond to the standards of our testing services. But, you know, the climate is different here, and products don't react the same way. You can trust us, we like Canada very much. I tried to do my imitation of Catherine again, and accept the rules of the game, and negotiate the way I was told to in the marketplace. Since we are in a marketplace here.

"I believe your laboratory will be able to work with ten samples."

The director dialled a number and discussed in the local language.

"The head of the laboratory says he can get along with three hundred doses."

"You don't have a laboratory, sir."

I wasn't expelled from Ivory Coast; I was repatriated. Catherine told me I had endangered relations between her NGO and both governments, and that the Canadian International Development Agency as well as the Canadian embassy wanted to have a more flexible-minded representative, one who was better versed in the local ways of doing business. For a little pleasure, I resigned myself to paying one hundred euros for a quick blow-job from Lolita, who told me it was an acceptable gift, but that university fees were increasing now that Whites were running the country. I thought she was attending a private business school.

17

That breach of contract earned me a letter of praise from my NGO. That was the compromise, and I said nothing about how I had rejected corruption, and the authorities did not mention my behaviour that was irregular at best, according to their code of conduct. That letter, international quotas, and my diplomas led me here, to The Hague. I have been a P2 Analyst in the Prosecutor's office for the last three years. I am at the International Criminal Court, I am thirty-one years old, and I believe in justice. One day, perhaps, I will put that asshole director who tried to steal five hundred doses of tritherapy in jail. Stealing people's health should be on the list of crimes against humanity.

18

Nothing is simple, especially justice.

19

The Hague suits me fine, but I don't care for its natives. The city is like me: patient and orderly. It suggests its personality, but does not assert it. It prefers to be discovered slowly. Lacking a spirit of adventure, I chose a neighbourhood – actually, a street – Denneweg, with its antique shops, fashionable stores, and restaurants. Patiently, I got to know the businesses and restaurants as if I were carrying out a meticulous investigation for the Court. In the process I made a few acquaintances I consider friends. Friends in exile will never be more than acquaintances.

In a hip street in the old town, there's a Chinese woman who sells Italian products. I wooed her stupidly and she pretended not to know, the way the Chinese government claims not to understand the concept of human rights. There are a number of antique shops with handsome naïve paintings that I would buy if I had a house and a wife. It's a wonderful thing, dreaming about that in front of a shop window. I love dreaming, even if I'm not romantic. And then there are the restaurants. I've been to just about all of them. Fiesta Latina, Maxime, Limon. I bring my files with me and hope to meet someone. Nothing happens, but I must admit I'm rather reserved. Next I go to a wine bar where the saddest people on earth meet. All men, important and wealthy. We talk about our lives elsewhere, our travels, and women pass like lightning flashes in the sky. Usually my last stop for the evening is at the Hothard, a floating bar on a canal that separates the French and the American embassies. I order a coffee, sink into my wicker chair, listen, and reflect. Sometimes the complexities of a file or palpitations whose causes remain unknown create anxiety that can be cured only with wine. Nothing serious.

Silence. No horns or squealing tyres or sirens. A quiet, orderly city, where calm and tranquility reign. A black duck with a white spot on its head, the same kind that starred in *The Ugly Duckling*, executes ten-metre sprints on the canal. In the sky, clouds moving with the same urgency flee the North Sea for the warmth of the continent. The bar rocks from time to time, and I feel I'm navigating down a peaceful thoroughfare. Along the canal, two rows of identical trees stand at identical height. The houses do not compete to stand out. Their facades are stern, but if you inspect them carefully, you can make out a detail or two, friezes, wrought iron ornamentation, the arrangement of the windows, the style of the doors, and even fake candles that beautify the entrances. These small personal touches, always discreet, tell the passer-by that all the houses were built on the same foundation, with the same need for solidity and light, with the same will to shelter the life behind the bricks from the gaze of outsiders, but that no-one will ever confuse two dwellings. They offer themselves like mannequins in the shop window wearing clothes from the same collection, but with different accessories. The Dutch are like their houses, conformist, expressing individuality in a few carefully chosen details. I don't much like the Dutch of The Hague.

We might be tempted to deduce from their architecture, the orderly nature of the landscape, and their social organization that the Dutchman is respectful of the environment, and is polite and sociable. The average Dutchman is the opposite of his country. And I include women in my generic Dutchman. The individual in question is noisy, vulgar, and impolite. Maybe because he's an incorrigible libertarian, but he doesn't believe that serving a customer requires a certain form of abnegation and respect. Here, the customer is a worker who has to labour to be served, and if he demands a little attention, more often than not he'll be insulted. On his bike, the Dutchman is a kamikaze who seeks out pedestrians and shouts *Banzai!* at the sight of a vessel to attack. On the sidewalk, the Dutchman forms a barrier with his bicycle, his stroller, his boyfriend or girlfriend. When you murmur "excuse me" to slip politely past him, he looks at you like you've invaded his country, and you quickly understand that it's better to simply step into the street. The Dutch resemble their climate. Violent gusts of wind, sudden rainstorms, persistent drizzle, low skies, and, at times, a little sun that hardly brightens their faces or makes them happier. Luckily, there are immigrants working in businesses and establishments. Indonesians, people from Sumatra and Surinam, warm, copper-hued smiles, though all of them speak that horrible, guttural, off-putting language known as Dutch.

But really, I'm not too unhappy, neither with the Dutch nor with my solitude. If I were in Brazil, I'd while away all my free time on the beach or listening to music. In France, I'd spend a fortune on restaurants. In Barcelona, I'd haunt Las Ramblas till late at night and eat a plate of fried fish at four in the morning. Back home in Montreal, I'd check out rue Saint-Denis, or avenue du Mont-Royal, or rue Saint-Viateur, knowing I'd meet friends, or at least acquaintances, and sharing a few secret codes with women on their own, a few references that would guide us through the labyrinth of relationships, in love or just for a night.

I take my pleasures that are not without their piquancy, even if they seem tiny, and I work the rest of the time. So much the better: what I'm accomplishing is important. I direct all my energy and thoughts to my mission, and sometimes I wonder whether a happy man could expend the same energy I do. I'm not unhappy, I'm just busy. And accomplishing important work. I'm sure of it.

20

Between the hotel and the building that houses the Court lies a pretty park with a canal where ducks and swans swim. The park is an illusion. When you leave it, two fifteen-storey white towers, as cold as icebergs, rise up in front of a noisy expressway. The building is intimidating at first glance, and my step was uncertain as I climbed the dozen steps that led to the revolving doors that opened onto a checkpoint like at the airport. The ID procedures and the photo for the magnetic card impressed me. I would be entering a place of importance, and at first I thought I had aimed too high. After my first meetings, I returned to the hotel in a state of nervous excitement. I didn't sleep all night. The next day, the prosecutor outlined my responsibilities with greater precision. I was to write position papers based on available information about Thomas Kabanga, a man I had never heard of, who was accused of conscripting and using child soldiers. Hundreds of UN documents, material from NGOs, video interviews with witnesses of the alleged crimes, newspaper articles, radio broadcasts – I had thousands of pages to read and millions of words to listen to. The work they were asking of me seemed outlandish. After a few meetings, as I walked down the long hallways to sign forms and confidentiality agreements, I realized I couldn't work in an environment like this. Too many pretty women, too beautiful and independent as Amazons, looking you in the eye and telling you "send me an e-mail" when you asked them out for a coffee in all innocence, to avoid another evening alone. Those women were too complicated for me. They spent their days immersed in crimes and exactions, and imagined the worst of others. I decided to move into the Mövenpick and work in my room. I told my superiors that I would be five minutes away by train if they wanted to meet with me. Financially, it made little sense, but I was freed from having to keep house. The hotel kept me from setting down roots, my life was elsewhere, and nothing came between me and my search for the truth about Thomas Kabanga.

21

I asked the hotel to take down the mirror over my worktable and I replaced it with a poster of Kabanga. When I sit down in front of my computer, I look at him and promise, "I'll get you, Kabanga." And when I start wondering what this is all about, I look at the poster. He's my age, and the first to be charged at the International Criminal Court, an accidental historical character, imprisoned here because he wanted too much and made all the wrong choices. Both of us are in the same stream of chance, he in history, and I in life. The more I look at him, the more I study him, the less sympathy I have, the fewer attenuating circumstances I can find for him. He is here because he wanted power. I am here because I have no power over life, only the ability to analyse the complexities of politics and its evolution, which has nothing to do with life. Compared to him, who destroyed thousands of lives, I'm a drone with no view of the future. Sometimes I feel inferior to him. I feared the violence of life. Kabanga cast himself into it. "He put his foot on the head of the screaming child and with his Rwandan boot he pushed down hard." We can't use that passage at the trial since neither witness nor document proves that the boot was Rwandan, and that the child had not committed some punishable offence. It's also impossible to prove that it was 'hard' or that the child was 'screaming'. This is not an easy job. I can see in the photo that the child is screaming, but that isn't enough. We all know he's guilty, but justice doesn't know that yet. I admit it: Kabanga fills my thoughts entirely. I am a monomaniac and might constitute a danger for society if this obsession was oriented toward any other human being. I live with this man. But he doesn't really obsess me; I never dream of him. I observe him, I analyse him, dissect him, manipulate him, weigh him, and question him the way a biochemist works on a promising molecule, frets over the initial results, but, trusting intuition, pursues the splitting of the molecule, combining it with other elements. In the eye of the microscope, all its beauty and complexity will appear, and then perhaps a new drug that might even save lives. The scientist who ends up winning the Nobel Prize isn't a man obsessed, he's just working, doing his job. That's what I'm doing with Kabanga. Stubbornly, I am doing my job.

He is a handsome man, and I can imagine that when he was young, his piercing eyes and determined features impressed the girls. We can't say it in the courtroom, but we do know it: Kabanga seduced every girl he came across. We have an interview with a certain Martine who maintains she bore his child. She states that Kabanga beat her when she showed him the beginnings of her belly. How could you beat a woman who is carrying your child? Youth can explain the inexplicable. I am searching for something human in him. I do not believe in absolute evil.

I thought I was being entrusted with the analysis of a major criminal, since the Court doesn't deal with petty thieves. I love that facile formulation. But Kabanga is a petty criminal, a very ordinary man responsible for very major crimes, crimes against humanity. I looked into his childhood. I was hoping for some indication, an event that would explain the path he took. But there was nothing, not a single clue from his childhood that would have turned him into a man whose destiny took him to a prison in The Hague. Rather vague and inconsistent testimony attests that he was either a brilliant student or a troublemaker, but never both at the same time. I look at his photo. The man is sure of himself; his eyes challenge the camera. But if you read his biography, you see he is completely mediocre. His actions are what make him exceptional. As a student he was smart enough to go on to college, but not smart enough to be accepted in a department like law that leads to the civil service, or politics or medicine that open the door to wealth. Kabanga chose the university in Kisangani and studies in psychology. That says a lot. He was more interested in the diploma than in a job. I make a note: "A need for recognition and status." In Africa, a university diploma, no matter its worth, automatically confers the status of intellectual to anyone who has one. A few accounts describe how, during his studies, Kabanga, in cafés and restaurants, claimed he was a psychologist and counselled patients for a few CFA francs under the table. We can't use that proof of intellectual dishonesty in the trial, but it would be worthwhile to inject small doses of it to make the judges understand that Kabanga is a cheat and a liar.

Obviously, in Bunia no-one consults a psychologist, especially one trained at the university in Kisangani. But his attendance in school, seminary, and university, and his diploma, his ability to speak in long sentences with psychological jargon impressed everyone he met. He was a gentleman for some, a complete rascal for others. He strutted and ravaged the female population of Bunia. I know that for a fact, we have testimony, he lifted his little finger and the waitress slipped into his bed, or the vendor in the market, or his boss's secretary. Is that testimony credible? Hard to say, since it's often the product of women seduced by Kabanga, then obviously disappointed not to have been chosen for his wife. When I compile and examine that material, I am abandoning the jurisdiction of the law. Kabanga's adventures are of no interest to the case I am working on. I am starting to settle the score at a distance with a man I despise. Emotions are disturbing the analysis.

I studied to become what I am: an analyst at the International Criminal Court. Kabanga studied to become a psychologist. If I sold shoes or was a taxi driver, I would feel frustration or a sense of failure. Not Kabanga. He went to university because he wanted to become an intellectual. He didn't choose psychology because he wished to ease the pain of the soul, or offer relief to children terrorized by legends or wars. He studied psychology because he couldn't do medicine or law. What interested him, a childhood friend testified, was power and money, especially the former. He sold dried beans and liked to talk prices with the Ugandan major in charge of supply, who explains to him that the gold market was more profitable. They become friends, since they shared the same habit of cheating their bosses. That's how wars are started. A major tells a psychologist that if he and his friends took control of the gold mines, everyone would get rich. The major pressed the point as girls circled around the two future Midases. They ate pizza and drank whisky in a restaurant owned by a Lebanese man who also had a gold trading business. Kabanga waved over Marguerite, a prostitute, and told her to come and join him later. Marguerite was positively thrilled. Night fell like a cloak of lead, suddenly, like a punch, a crushing blow. Karim, the Lebanese guy, sat down. "Thomas, all the Hema businessmen have their own militias, a few dozen armed men, why not get them together and fix the land problem with the Lendu once and for all? You know how to talk, people respect you, the Ugandans trust you." The major nodded his head and added, "You form a party, you get those people together, we'll train you, and you take control of Ituri, then we divide it up, the diamonds, the gold, and the coltan." The three of them drank a bottle of Johnnie Walker Black and slapped each other on the back. Marguerite was impatient. She told Kabanga she wanted to leave. The psychologist got up slowly, walked over to her, and knocked her out with a heavy, powerful punch to the jaw. Then he sat down and ordered another bottle of whisky. We know the woman never got up, but Kabanga will not be judged for that murder. It isn't covered by the Rome Statute, but by local criminal justice.

I don't like the man. I don't respect him, he has no intellectual qualities or true political project. But out of concern for justice and equality, I try to find extenuating circumstances for him. I search and search, I reflect, I analyse, and I can find only one that speaks to my Western mind: poverty. But goddammit, all Africa is poor, so all Africans have the right to become criminals. That doesn't cut it. And besides, he wasn't really poor. He was able to finance his studies. I don't believe the man is a twisted criminal, a monster, a serial killer like Hannibal Lecter in *The Silence of the Lambs*. Those people are psychopaths, madmen, psychiatric cases. No, Tom – I use that familiar tone with him as I work on his file – committed crimes the way a bureaucrat or a government employee fills out forms or closes his wicket in front of a long line of waiting people so he can take his coffee break. He was not moved by irrepressible impulses or uncontrollable fantasies. Crime was not the objective in itself, but a tool, a mechanism to get what he wanted. That makes him more repulsive to me. An ordinary man, thousands dead, three thousand child soldiers. All of it carried out, thought through, organised with absolute cool-headedness, with no real hatred, and no emotion. The coldness of crime, biting and cutting like a February blizzard.

I have a separate file called 'Rape'. If I take all the testimony seriously, Kabanga raped a woman a week for two years. If one of the girl soldiers had witnessed a rape, we would have been able to use this aspect against him. But that's not the case. The two girls who are going to testify will describe how they were kidnapped, then forced into combat, and with one of them, forced to wrap electric wire around the testicles of a prisoner and squeeze until they popped out. She cried so much when she told that story that the prosecutor wasn't sure she'd make a useful witness. I've accumulated thousands of such things in my files and memos about Kabanga, but very little of it will be admissible in court. Justice is not concerned with malicious personalities, and judges are not there to reflect on the qualities or faults of the accused, only on his responsibility for the crimes.

The man is cruel and basically worthless. He took pleasure in dominating and humiliating people for no apparent reason. His malice obsesses me, it's a form of pettiness, mediocrity, like filth, human garbage. I am not thinking of the serious crimes he is accused of, but his behaviour on a daily basis – Kabanga in his life as a normal man, the businessman, the customer in a restaurant, the lover and husband, in his relations with domestics and people in the street.

Testimony of Marie, a waitress:
"I am a student. It was my first day at work as a waitress. Mr. Kabanga came in and asked me to move three customers who were eating at his favourite table. I told him I couldn't do that. He called me a whore and went to see my boss, who agreed to his request immediately. His two bodyguards were boys who were thirteen or fourteen, I knew them from school. They called me a whore too. He ordered an American pizza. I don't know the difference between pizzas. The one I served him wasn't the one he ordered. He grabbed my wrist and twisted it so hard I thought it would break. Then he went

to see my boss in his office. I was fired on the spot. In the street, his bodyguards grabbed me by the arm and led me to his house. Mr. Kabanga showed me to Commander Komo and Commander Komo raped me."

In that testimony, the only thing with legal importance is the two child soldiers. All the rest disgusts me. There was no witness to the rape, but I believe her.

The 11:59 pm train. Sometimes distress overcomes me and I picture myself in a train taking me to someone I would love tenderly, the right way, the way women want to be loved. Sometimes I imagine a house, a child crying, a little yard. Sometimes I think of happiness. Then I go back to work.

Though he was eloquent and self-confident, Kabanga suffered from an enormous social inferiority complex. In Bunia, the big businessmen and the powerful landowners are Hema from the south. Kabanga came from the north.

Testimony of Aristide, one of Kabanga's employees:

"When he came to Bunia after his studies, he only had his diploma and his fine way of speaking. He knew a lot of handsome words. He visited the merchants and the heads of the Hema community. 'Don't you see the Lendu are going to take control of the region? They're united, while we're divided. We need to unite the Hema of Ituri and retake control of our land, our gold, and our coltan.' Until then the merchants were happy just to count their profits and pay off the judges when there was a conflict. Each had his own armed guards made up of unemployed, bored young men who waved around their pistols to impress the crowd. Kabanga said he would turn those little groups into a national militia, and train them, make real soldiers out of them, so the Ugandan occupiers would understand that he was the only man they needed to talk to, and that way they would stop playing the Hema against the Lendu. The Ugandans, you understand, sir, were in our country to keep the peace, but you can't eat peace. They were out to take our wealth. Everybody has always wanted to steal our wealth and everybody has always succeeded. Look at how we live in this province of gold and diamonds. And the whole Congo is like that, a rich country whose riches leave on a long journey. Kabanga told the commander he could form an army that would serve Uganda. Kabanga was negotiating with both sides. He took money from the merchants and from the Ugandans. That's how he started his dried bean business and his gold exchange, and then one day he announced in the newspaper that the Congolese Patriotic Union had been founded, it was going to form a regular army and demand autonomy for the province. Kabanga was enjoying himself immensely. When he came home a little drunk from his rounds in town, he would chortle and describe how everyone was eating out of his hand, and how he was manipulating all of them, the Ugandans and the Hema, especially the ones from the south who considered themselves superior. But he would have them licking his boots, it was only a matter of time. He pointed to a dead mosquito on the table. 'Aristide, are you asleep or what? What's that thing doing on my table? Come here. Lick it up!' I washed the table with my tongue as he made jokes. 'It doesn't taste as good as a woman, but it's better than nothing. Anyway, that's what you are – nothing.' Madame Kabanga tried to kill him because he humiliated her so badly, he made her do the job of a domestic. He told her to get naked and soap herself up and wash the floor with her breasts and her belly. He laughed and laughed as she rubbed the floor and he laughed even harder when the bullet missed him. 'Can't even shoot straight, a real woman.' He beat her to his heart's content and threw her out the door, naked. 'You'll find a taker dressed like that, for sure.' Madame Kabanga was quickly replaced by a girl he humiliated in a thousand ways that I don't wish to describe because the thought of it offends me. Why did I stay in his employ? Sir, it's obvious you come from a long way away. I had a job and the boss paid on time. Humiliation is part of life like the sun that almost always shines, like crickets and poverty. When you're African, if you want to survive, you have to be philosophical about it."

I understand their words, but they don't resonate in my heart. That's because I know nothing of real pain, humiliation, and resignation. I know nothing of the world's tragedy in my flesh. I am an analyst, a witness, a sort of interface. How should I live? The last train has passed. It must be three o'clock in the morning.

Testimony of Josué:

"I was selling cigarettes in front of the Lebanese restaurant where Mr. Kabanga would come and eat on the patio. I had no desire to sell cigarettes, but my parents took me out of school. They didn't have enough money. I thought I might make enough to go back to school. I sold lighters and condoms too, but only the Whites bought condoms. My dream was to play rap music. We started a group, we recorded a tape, and I would sell it with my cigarettes. Mr. Kabanga had turned into a boss. He was always surrounded by his young bodyguards, some of them were my friends and they showed me their Kalashnikovs, they liked to play with the safety. I didn't envy them because the only thing I wanted was to make music and get to Kinshasa somehow. Do you know MC Solaar? That day, Mr. Kabanga was having dinner with a big Ugandan military man. He came and bought a pack of Marlboros. 'You're Josué, I know who you are, your parents owe me money. You'll have to work for me to pay back their debt.' He didn't even give me the money for the cigarettes. Then he took my whole carton. That's how I became what you call a child soldier. At first, it wasn't too hard. We did exercises like at school, we crawled under barbed wire, we scaled little walls made out of logs, and we sang songs about how the Lendu were the devil. They gave us rifles made of wood, we marched up and down, and we listened to nasty speeches about the Lendu. I didn't know they ate Hema children. We were pretty proud of ourselves, we were well fed, and we were with our friends. I figured the money would show up soon, so I didn't worry. The first time we fired our Kalashnikovs, I realized it was serious and that we weren't kids anymore. At the start we aimed at tree trunks, just to learn how to handle the rifle, how to hold it correctly so it would be stable. Then they set up straw men fifty metres away. I was a good shot, the Ugandan instructors told me. A short burst and the straw man completely disintegrated, he flew into a thousand pieces, everywhere. I trembled as I wondered if it would do the same thing to someone like me, who's a lot more solid than a straw man. Yes, it does the same thing. I saw it once during the attack to take control of the goldmines. I shot and a human being did the same thing as the straw man. Both arms up in the air, his body thrown backward, pieces of flesh flying every-where. I hope I didn't kill anyone else. But then I did worse and I still can't sleep because of it. Mr. Kabanga told me to shoot a prisoner in the anus and I did. Every night, I hear him howling like a hyena caught in a trap of sharp sticks that doesn't kill him right away, but makes him suffer and die slowly. If you have to kill, you should do it fast. I ran away. When I went back to my parents' village, everything had been destroyed. I found an old uncle who hadn't moved, he was still living in his burned hut, and he told me my parents were ashamed of me, they had repudiated me. I love my parents, and what I did, I did for them, and since I can't tell them that, I'll tell you, sir, and maybe they'll hear me, I don't know, on the radio or the TV. The radio would be better. My father has a transistor. But I think I'll never be able to play music again."

22

It's three o'clock in the morning. Every time I re-read Josué's testimony, I cry. I don't even have a picture of him. I don't know if he's big or little, skinny or well built, but I love him. I'd like to listen to his tape. At the trial, they won't reveal even his first name. Only how old he was at the time of the events. He will never have his moment of truth out in the open. We have to protect the witnesses, it's an obsession here. There are maybe a dozen of us at the Court who know his first name. At least Josué will be able to look Kabanga in the eye – it won't be easy for a victim to do that – and say, "You stole my life from me, Mr. Kabanga. I was a child, and now I'm not anything at all." No, that's not what he'll say, and if he did, the defence would object and the judges would sustain. Stealing a childhood is not a crime. Josué won't understand why he can't just tell the truth the way he saw it, the plain truth. He won't understand either why Kabanga is as well dressed as ever, while he's dressed like a Bunia cigarette vendor, just a little better than the others, maybe. He'll wonder about all this palaver and putting on airs and why White men in suits are questioning him as if he were the criminal. Poor children, whom we will subject to the torture of the law and not the liberation of justice.

I'm getting carried away and I know it. I am departing from my methodical, rational approach. How do you reconcile the search for truth with legalities? It is the first time I've asked myself that question, the first time I think that statutes and procedures and legal guidelines don't guarantee the administration of justice. What if law were only an intellectual exercise with no relation to what is just, decent, and self-evident? Kabanga is guilty. Hundreds of thousands of people experienced his guilt in their flesh. Why do we have to prove beyond a reasonable doubt, like in an ordinary murderer's trial? And whose reasonable doubt – that of thousands of victims, or of three cold-eyed, distant judges who have never set foot in Ituri?

23

The telephone rang. "Can I come over?"

Myriam and I have come to an agreement. She distrusts men, and women have always made my life complicated. One evening after pizza, as we were walking down Herenstraat in Voorburg, we turned in the direction of my hotel. We didn't say much, but we knew we were going to fuck. The only thing in our lives that reassures us is sex. In the elevator, we didn't kiss. We looked at the ground. Myriam saw the photo of Kabanga. She went through the room, looking for someplace to sit. Finally she chose the armchair in front of my worktable. Myriam came from Somalia, but studied in Kansas, and hasn't visited her country for ten years. She doesn't like being Somali. She wants Dutch citizenship and has been taking crash courses in the language. Myriam wants to become someone else. I'm happy being me; I'm familiar with all my ins and outs.

I grasped for a subject of conversation. I wanted to go back to the light-hearted atmosphere we had before. "You can go on the other bed, I feel tired." I sat down on one of the beds. We had lost all familiarity with the act of love, we searched for each other, and hesitated. We had no skill and sense of ease in this complex exercise, and that made us laugh. Myriam has a pretty smile and I think that's what excited me, her smile, more than her long graceful body, more than her small breasts. We managed to make love well enough.

The next morning, Myriam left before I awoke. She sent me an e-mail that afternoon. "Let's make a deal. We'll see each other when we need sex. No questions, no attachments."

"Agreed," I answered.

She returned a few days later. Like the first evening, she looked for somewhere to sit. She chose the foot of my bed. She seemed nervous, anxious, full of troubling thoughts. The last train had passed, it was 2:45 a.m. Sleep, all I could think of was sleep. "Claude, I think I love you." I don't want to be loved, and I don't want to love. I didn't have the time or the availability. But Myriam had her charms. At first I saw only her timid smile, but now the grace of her body held me, and how wonderfully light she was as she lay upon me. When two people meet, they control nothing but their own defences. I was circumspect, distant, timid, and humble, and I was able to calm her fear of men. I proved that men could be trustworthy. If I hadn't been a Court analyst, if I wasn't tasked with tracking down the planet's worst criminals, I could have tried passion and loving with abandon, the upsetting of reason that, as soon as it occurs, fills every part of the brain and casts the lover into constant disquiet and uncertainty. Later, maybe I would try to love Myriam, but not now, not three days from the beginning of Kabanga's trial.

Myriam was part of the team of jurists who wrote up the judges' decisions. She was a judge's ghostwriter, in this case the ghost of Judge Fulton, an arrogant, perverse Englishman. We never spoke of Kabanga; professional discretion forbid it. The prosecutor didn't like Fulton's concept of the law, full of codicils, commas, and obtuse rules, and the judge had contempt for the prosecutor's idea of justice that was based as much on law as on equity, but also on the accounts of the victims, the uproar of the planet, and other such factors. We both understood the conflict between these two irreconcilable visions of justice, but we avoided the discussion that could shake, if not completely break, our relationship.

I searched. How could I say yes and no, or no and yes, both at the same time, to this declaration of love that put me ill at ease? I couldn't do it. I always say either yes or no; ambiguous arrangements are foreign to me, and lies repulsive.

Myriam's body was a graceful dark serpent on the white sheet. She looked at me with eyes like a vulture. "Claude, Kabanga is going to be freed because of a procedural error. The prosecutor knows. That's why your mission to Bunia was cancelled. The decision will be announced on Monday and Kabanga will go back to his country if he wants to."

I asked her to repeat it, but that was only something you say to make sure your heart is still beating and that you're still breathing. She didn't repeat it, she only said, "Claude, come to me" with such sweetness and sadness in her voice that I lay down next to her, as close as I could, and let her hold me in her loving arms that seemed like the wings of a bird, protecting me.

Our team had imagined every possible outcome, an exemplary sentence, but also a lighter sentence, and we even considered with a laugh of disbelief that Kabanga might be acquitted, but never freed before trial. One hundred thousand people know in their flesh and through their pain that the man is a criminal. But the judge didn't give a damn. And what a judge, all gung ho in his own country, an artist of maximum sentences, a grand master of the rule of law. I felt like crying, or screaming, but I was paralysed, wrapped in this loving body like a larva, a parasite, a thing with no consistence. Myriam ran her hands gently through my hair. "Claude, the judge is totally full of himself. I know him. His only thought is for his reputation as a great legal mind."

Our team knew that, but we never imagined that the very high esteem he had for himself would lead him to invoke a procedural error as a way of freeing a criminal.

We had confidential documents from the UN and members of local NGOs. These documents were used to build a case against Kabanga. The judge ordered us to share them with the defence. Had we obeyed him, we would have endangered people's lives. So we sent over only the essential parts. The judge knew that, but didn't give a damn. For him it was all or nothing. The man wanted to write the history of international law and had no interest in justice.

"You have to sleep, Claude, you need to sleep." Her voice was as soft as the summer breeze. I was less afraid of her love. I had no romantic feelings towards her, only the sense of comfort she brought me, like a warm bath or a fresh sheet, gentle to the touch. I could get used to her love if she didn't demand my own.

24

Myriam left. The rain is beating at the windowpane, the malicious, perverse Dutch rain. I am drinking the instant coffee that mid-range hotels offer their guests, a kind of syrup that conjures up the idea of coffee. Strangely, I wish Myriam were here. Or someone else who could explain why I have this feeling that I've wasted my life, why the freeing of Kabanga has turned my patient apprenticeship of the world into something useless. Kabanga, freed, destroys me. Maybe Myriam could tell me why, or Claus or Pascal. I don't seem to know myself. I don't, and it's a great revelation to me that only a woman could understand that life has no further interest for me. Why a woman? Because women are mothers.

Testimony of Béatrice:
"Mr. Kabanga came into the house with three bodyguards who were students at the same school I went to. He asked Mother if she was a good Hema and if she thought that all Hema families should work for the supremacy of the Hema over the Lendu. Mother said yes. That's how I became a soldier. I wasn't taken away or kidnapped, and nothing violent happened to me. Mother ordered me to be a soldier. I didn't like anything about war. During training, when I shot at the targets with my Kalashnikov, I shook and I trembled. I was a very bad soldier. That's why, during my first attack, the Lendu took me prisoner. I lost count of how many times they raped me. I finally managed to escape. I went back to my mother's house and told her everything. She threw me out. I went to see my Hema uncles and cousins, but

they turned me away too. I am impure now, full of Lendu sperm. I am eighteen years old and I work as a prostitute in the Lebanese restaurant, mostly for foreigners. I know I'll never get married and never have children. I love children, but when I go up to one in the street or the market, the parents grab him and pull him away from me as if I had the plague. That's what Mr. Kabanga did to me. I hope you are going to punish him."

No, Béatrice, we are not going to punish him. An insane judge who knows nothing of your despair, and who spends his time reading procedure manuals, is leading a crusade against the UN to prove that only judges are judges, they're demi-gods, masters of this earth, that their status gives them the right to forget that you'll never have children, or if you do it'll be the fruit of a relationship contracted at the Lebanese restaurant, and you'll abort it because the father is a Belgian soldier who slapped you across the face when you admitted you were pregnant.

No, Béatrice, this Court will do nothing for you. The Court is concerned only with its own future existence. It is using you to create jurisprudence, rules, and procedures that one day might give the Béatrices of the future the chance to demand and receive justice. No, Béatrice, don't expect anything from The Hague. For the judges, you are a hamster on a wheel of endless sadness, a guinea pig whose DNA is being tested for what is just and what is not.

Béatrice, I am going to go to Bunia to say that I'm sorry in the name of the Court. Thanks to your extensive testimony, I discovered that you wanted to be a nurse, that you're HIV-positive, and that you've had two abortions. I love you, Béatrice.

25

Kabanga's lawyer is speaking to the press. He's perorating. Meanwhile, Kagamé, the President of Rwanda, must be preparing to welcome his friend Kabanga who delivered him diamonds, gold, and coltan. The Western media are ecstatic over the audacious and remarkable concept of justice that holds sway in The Hague. International justice is perfect, flawless even. The future biographies of the judges won't be bothered with these facts: the search for perfection kills people, frees criminals, creates shock waves in countries that are already unstable – who cares? Reading the world press casts me into a despair that has nothing theoretical about it. Now that Kabanga is free, my life is slipping away, like blood dripping slowly from a wound next to the heart. I was asked to 'write a few lines', polite, prefabricated formulas that put a decent set of clothes on defeat and failure. I try, but can't. My ability to analyse and synthesize disappeared with Kabanga. Astonishingly, I discovered anger, rage, real revolt, rejection of the established order, of the rules and conventions that once governed me. And if these emotions are so strong and so clear, they must have been in me all the while, and I was denying them, I was wrapping them carefully in sheets of silk paper known as pragmatism and my rational method, I was filing them away as if they were items of objective information. What if I'd used the same care to wrap up everything that involved feelings, in order to avoid distress, uncertainty, and pain? I was a coward. Kabanga never knew fear and he was free. He could become the emperor of Bunia once more. When you're like me, you don't decide to change and free yourself, you understand that the process has been completed a long time ago, and you accept that transformation without worrying about the consequences. You let yourself be carried by the great tide that will erode the oldest granite cliffs in the world and modify the landscape forever.

26

"Myriam, I'm quitting."

27

Myriam displayed her slender grace in my room. I'm free, which allows me to say what I think instead of scribbling my thoughts down on sheets of paper I'll throw away the next day. I no longer fear rejection because I know where I'm going: I'm going to Bunia.

"Myriam, I don't love you the way I think you love me."

"You don't know anything about love and even less about Africans. So you don't know anything about the love I have for you."

"I love your smile and I love making love with you more and more, but that's not love."

"What if I loved you because you're respectful and gentle with me, and that's good enough? Would you say that's love the way you see it?"

"No. I'd say it's affection, a sort of mutual trust."

"What if, for me, mutual trust was all the happiness I could expect from a man? Would you agree that my feeling is as deep as what you call love?"

Myriam was slipping through the cracks in me opened up by Kabanga. If I was giving in to anger and rage, it meant there was room in me for other just as unreasonable feelings: affection, desire, and, who knows, love. But I'm not there yet, in that new world of emotions, where I am a mere apprentice, fearful and hesitant. I needed to find my bearings.

"So we could go away together."

When you're afraid of feelings and you finally let go, you don't have the right words to express them. I just said the worst thing you could imagine. I went and got a whisky from the minibar.

Myriam smiled and opened her arms to me.

"That's a nice image. Come to me, Claude."

I lay down next to her, and like the teenager I once was, I looked, and desired.

"In your country, the roads people travel are short. In my country, they are long."

We made love as if preparing a long journey, slowly and delicately. We found a shared rhythm based on her past pain and my shyness. It was as slow as the tide that moves toward the peacefully sleeping land, that is unaware of the great changes in store. We have changed. We looked each other in the eye, and didn't hide in each other's shoulder when the sharp thrust of pleasure came. We began to talk. Small words, ordinary sentences that were like poetry to me, "That's good," "Again," "Go slow," "Yes!" We shared conversation and laughter after sex. We were, I believe, in love in a friendly kind of way.

Myriam fell asleep with her head on my shoulder. I have a woman for the first time in my life. Her calm, smooth breathing and absolute trust as she slept next to me, a stranger, convinced me of that. When I say, "I have a woman," I'm not talking about possession. It means that a woman is my companion, and she can say to herself, "I have a man," too. But why the fear and anxiety, why the palpitations and shortness of breath, the sweaty palms and scalding forehead? I calmed down the way a tropical storm blows itself out. I knew the answer very well. At thirty-five, I was finally becoming a man and agreeing to enter life, real life that is, as a French doctor put it, "a fatal disease sexually transmitted by humans". I want to be with Myriam, but I don't love her.

She always disappeared before I woke up. This morning, she was here. She had gone to the dining room and brought back croissants and *café au lait*. We didn't speak. This first breakfast together unfolded like a ritual, a ceremony, in absolute silence. She took a shower; the sound of the water delighted me because I knew which body the droplets were caressing. She dried her hair and turned to me with a shy smile. She got dressed. A woman getting dressed is often more desirable than one who is taking off her clothes.

"Claude, I'm going to quit too."

"Will you come to Bunia with me?"

"That's a long road that interests me."

I don't know why, but without thinking about it for a second, I asked her to come to Bunia with me. I admit I don't understand, but it doesn't really matter. If I asked, it's because I wanted to. She left. I missed her already, and she hadn't even reached the elevator. I must have spent about twelve thousand days building up my personality, consciously, over the last twelve years, deliberately. Feelings, emotion, and desire break down reason. I built my life as an adult on ideas, principles, and convictions. I couldn't take much credit, though, since the uncontrollable impulses of the soul, the sweat breaking out on the skin for no apparent reason, the eyes delighted by the sight of a beautiful body – those things only ever led me to failure and incomprehension. Life didn't terrorize me to the point that I withdrew. Women did.

Then everything changed because of Kabanga. Strange. I decided to accept my failure to understand.

I let myself go and discovered what it was like to live without a net, how fear can disappear. I'm not afraid to be that tightrope walker; I fear neither anger nor desire.

I said *Bunia* without thinking it over, without knowing what I would do there, and why exactly I wanted to go. But when I spoke the name, I knew I needed to be there to witness Kabanga's return to the place he terrorized, to watch him be free.

My resignation was greeted with expressions of regret

I refused to analyse. I turned in my magnetic ID card to security. The Dutch civil servant didn't even look at me. The Dutch have this special talent for looking at you without seeing you. I sat in the park in front of the Court, on my favourite bench, the one most favoured by the ducks and swans. They approach it sometimes when the young want to take a rest on the grass. I will miss my ducks, but not the Dutch. I have read plenty of Dutch novelists, the celebrated Helle Haase, the troublemaker, Jeroen Brouwers, and especially Harry Mulisch. I read, hoping to discover some virtues in this country. I am used to reading literature inspired by love of country, as is the case in Quebec and France. I was fed on idiotic national glorification, "the authentic Quebec nature", "Quebec creativity", "French genius", as if the Chinese hadn't invented gunpowder and the Arabs, optometry and algebra. Those authors confirmed it: the Dutch smile does not exist; it is a grimace learned at business school. No more than Dutch hospitality exists, which can be summed up as the permission accorded the customer to sit down in a restaurant and wait for a menu, and if he asks a question about a certain dish, he deserves an accusing look and service at the speed of a snail. Holland is the most civilized of the barbaric countries. How had I managed to live here for three whole years? You have to be dead or Dutch to survive in this place. And the language, the constant spewing of guttural sounds, that way of shouting, emitting Gs gnawed on by the Rs that follow, it all sounds like belching that would insult any normal pair of ears. I hate this country. I took the full measure of my hatred sitting on the bench with my ducks that don't quack like the Dutch; they are too timid and polite. I'd like to have an average Dutchman sitting here with me so I could tell him what I think of his country. I've been thinking it, and now I'd like to say it out loud.

And I'd like to tell him what I feel. That's new. When I went back to the hotel, the concierge gave me a knowing smile. At the restaurant, Michael said, "Hello, sir," and the lovely Edith pretended not to see me because she didn't want to say no to an invitation I'd issued six months ago.

"Michael, do you like me?"

"What do you mean, sir?"

"Do you want to know more about who I am?

"I don't have time for human contact, I am working."

Michael turned his back to me and concentrated on the handball game on TV.

Myriam. I love thinking of her. And I don't believe I've fallen into a teenage emotional maelstrom. I'm calm and peaceful, stripped of excessive emotion. She told me she'd pack her things and be here at nine in the evening. I don't look at my watch; I know she'll be here. I glanced at the handball game. Michael picked his nose. A scent of jasmine. It was nine o'clock. Is happiness the peace that comes with certainty? Maybe. She's there. Myriam has become Somali again. She was wearing traditional dress and a scarf that's not Muslim, but Somali, it must be for protection against sandstorms, or maybe it was just embellishment, vanity. She was dragging two enormous suitcases in which all her tight-fitting jeans must be tucked away, since that was the only thing she wore during her stay at the Court. Strangely, she was not smiling, and she didn't even look at me. Myriam kept her eyes on the carpet and stood unmoving, the very image of a respectful woman awaiting her husband's orders.

"Is that an Islamic scarf?"

"For certain women it is, but for me it's Somali. It keeps me warm when the darkness falls like a veil, and I think it's pretty. It frames my face very well. I think I'm beautiful with the scarf. So you see, it's not a scarf to hide behind. The prettier the scarf is, the better it frames the face, the more men desire you. That's why when I came to the West, because I wanted nothing more of the desires of men, I dressed in the Western style."

"You want to come upstairs?"

She smiled. "Yes, we will be better in our place."

Our place. I wasn't so sure, even if her words did give me pleasure.

Her two suitcases weren't stuffed with jeans after all, but books, treatises on law, files, NGO, and UN reports. She glided through the room, tidied the books scattered here and there, picked up the ashtray, emptied it, washed it, and placed it on the night table. If I pictured angels, this would be how they moved, with absolute ease, and grace both delicate and self-assured. I lay down on the bed to watch her. She knew as much because, from time to time, she would lower her head and smile shyly. "You don't mind?" And she went back to her work, arranging and putting away my things with meticulous care. "Your shirts are all wrinkled. I'll see to that tomorrow." She glanced around the room to make sure everything was in its place. "All that's missing is flowers."

Flowers? Wait, I'll be right back. An extensive garden centre stood next to the hotel. I climbed onto the hotel kitchen's trash bins pushed up against the centre's fence. From there it was child's play, even if three years of hotel living and file-reading, three years of a totally sedentary life had atrophied my once-athletic muscles. In the darkness, I chose randomly, a rosebush lit by the cold September moon that seemed to bear flowers as white as bed sheets. The Dutch are vulgar and have no taste, but they have invented the most beautiful flowers in the world, who knows how. They weren't exactly white, but ecru with a green hue at the very tip and again at the heart of the petals, the flowers a harmonious echo of their stems. Myriam admired them. "You stole this." No, I borrowed it and I'll go back tomorrow and pay. She smiled.

"I'm tired," she said.

"So am I."

She turned off the light and sat on the bed. Slowly, she undressed. A moonbeam shone upon her. I looked with admiration. This would not be like a wedding night, it would be a time of trust and tranquility, that was what I hoped for. Could we fall asleep together, at the same time, breathing at the same rhythm as we slept, dreaming the same dream, moving in harmony without the body of one disturbing the body of the other? Could we be corpses in the same tomb, united in the repose of the soul and the body?

Yes, we could. I floated as if on the sea, in the half-sleep we always try and prolong. A warm arm lay across my shoulders. I took the hand at the end of that arm. A finger of that hand clasped one of my fingers. We were awake. Waking can be a process of discovery and apprehension of the world. Her slim legs wrapped around mine, and I understood she wasn't just obeying some reflex as she slept. This was an invitation. I turned to her slightly. Myriam was looking at me, her eyes heavy with sleep. And even if I didn't see all the depth, the pain, and at the same time all the sweetness of the world in them, I did see eyes that wanted me. We made love slowly and gently, without speaking, as if we were on a ship carried by calm seas and clement winds.

Myriam made the coffee.

"I'll go pay for the flowers."

At the gardening centre, I discovered a red-faced, heavy woman who looked at me with Dutch circumspection as I confessed to my larceny. She smelled of the earth she worked with, and her nails were black. I showed her a rosebush that looked like the one I borrowed. She grasped my elbow like a schoolmarm catching a pupil red-handed. I heard the black ducks quacking, and the cold wind rose and drove a penetrating drizzle into our faces. "You should have borrowed that one, sir." Yellow, golden orange, and pink, the petals at the base opened like lace. In the centre, they formed a tight cone. Fragility of lace petals and the solid heart of a flower. I had never really looked at a flower. I had never looked at anything closely except the breasts in my childhood dictionary and the black ducks on my canal. I promised to return the borrowed rosebush, and now I had a new one, a luminous, splendid, luxurious rose, eight flowers and seven buds, the children of flowers that are like jewels, or sculptures.

Myriam went to get croissants, fruit, and cheese. She found a white cloth and set the table like in a proper house. I contemplated my room. Everything was in perfect order. I would have never done that, but I liked it and I also liked Myriam's eagerness to serve me, and ask me what I want. I felt at home.

"Now what do we do?"

28

Several issues were hiding behind the apparently simple question she asked with no visible emotion, as she dipped a piece of chocolate roll into her *café au lait.* "Let's go for a walk." I was avoiding her banal question that was not banal at all. I've never cared for walking. It's an exercise that combines contemplation and boredom and has no objective at all, practiced by old men who don't like television and lonely people who distrust life. I don't remember ever having walked without a goal in mind: a corner store, a market, a meeting place. My steps must produce tangible results. You don't walk for no reason. I decided to turn onto Herenstraat and inspect the shop windows, then go as far as the big park at the end of the street, and see what that outsized, baroque, white pavilion in the middle of it was about.

Concealed behind Myriam's simple question was everything I did not yet understand and that frightened me, despite my happiness. What do we do? We, you and me. What will we do tomorrow, you and I? What's the plan for us, you and me? It's not the future that concerned me, it's this thing called 'us' we were creating, that I desired as much as I feared.

"We'll go for a walk, it's nice out. There's a park at the end of Herenstraat."

That was what she wanted. I knew that in the park in front of the white pavilion, she would watch the pond and without looking my way, ask, "Now what do we do?" The only original street in Voorburg that called itself "the village" was of no interest at all with its shabby stores. I discovered that the white pavilion was a

Gil Courtemanche

somewhat chic restaurant patronized by hefty, middle-age Dutch ladies and red-faced accountants. The swans on the pond gave the place a touch of elegance, and the old oak trees, some distinction. Except for my black ducks, I never thought of looking at birds or animals with any sense of pleasure – let alone trees. "Now what do we do?" I knew it. The question would return constantly like a mantra, or a verse from the Koran. "We'll go back to the hotel." "Okay, but tomorrow, and the day after tomorrow, next week, next month, next year...?"

I liked Myriam very much. I didn't want to tell her that Kabanga had pushed me into her arms, that Kabanga being freed had laid me down on top of her, and that anger helped me discover the desire to live, and not her small breasts and her shy smile, though those things drew me to her. I couldn't imagine myself without her now. The tree I admired was because of her. Otherwise I'd be in my room ruminating or consulting my files. I was less afraid, but still untrusting. Happiness was like a springtime flower.

She took my hand and held it tight. I had to answer her.

"We're going to live in Bunia."

Maybe I went too far. *We're going to live in Bunia.* I should have said, "We'll go and visit Bunia." For now, we're going to live in the Mövenpick a few more days so I can finish the complex transactions that await me. Transferring my money to a bank that has relations with the Congo, with the promise that I'll be able to access my funds there. I have no intention of strolling around with thousands of dollars in cash in my pocket.

The *us* was settling in, and this personal pronoun worried me, despite how often it was used. "Let's go to Martin's place, the wine bar, you can meet my old companions in solitude." Those companions tended to be homosexual, and discreet since they were civil

116

servants or diplomats or judges, but they did have an eye for women. They recognized beauty and grace in an instant and were effusive with their compliments when I introduced Myriam. She played the game much better than I did, since I never knew what to say when someone paid me even the ghost of a compliment. They asked about her clothes, and she twirled and made her long dress dance, then put on the timid, feminine look of a Somali woman in a foreign land. It was an act for the benefit of White men. Other men's eyes on Myriam comforted and delighted me. I could see it and feel it, she was watching me like a fawn hiding in a thicket. What fear can be born of admiration? I asked Martin as we smoked a cigarette in the doorway of his bar. Martin had that beauty that aging men have when they retain their elegance and wisdom, and sometimes he spoke of his secret garden, which he recalled without going into detail. "The fear of love, Claude. But I think you are in love." Myriam had stopped smiling. The customers were cackling away, and she shot me a desperate look. We took the last train to Voorburg. The car was dirty, the train noisy, and a group of punks amused themselves by terrorizing the passengers. I held her hand and she put her head on my shoulder, and if the trip had been longer than four minutes, I think she would have fallen asleep. I don't know if I was in love the way Martin thought, but I know I have a woman for the first time in my life. *Have a woman.* Do women say 'have a man'? I don't think so.

29

(Reuters) "The Supreme Court of the Democratic Republic of the Congo has found against the opinion of the government that Thomas Kabanga may return to his native country. Accused by the International Criminal Court of war crimes and crimes against humanity, in particular the systematic recruitment of child soldiers, the leader of the Congolese Patriotic Union was freed on a procedural matter. The judges decided that the rules pertaining to full disclosure to the defence were not respected by the prosecution. This decision, which set off shock waves at the UN and among NGOs working in the area of international justice, has put into question the very existence of the Court. The prosecutor's office, in order to carry out its investigations, must work with civil society in regions where there are conflict situations, but the NGOs demand a certain amount of confidentiality, since their members could be subject to reprisals. The prosecutor declared that he was bitterly disappointed by the judges' decision."

Radio Okapi, DRC: "Two young men from Bunia as well as a man working for the International Criminal Court were killed this morning as they were heading for the ICC offices in Kinshasa. They were ambushed in front of the Ministry of Justice. Sources say that the two men, one of whom is known as Maurice, were protected witnesses in the Kabanga affair. The Court ordered that Kabanga be freed a week ago, and we know that the former leader of the CPU is preparing to return to the country. Our correspondent in Bunia reports that military garb and weapons have reappeared on the streets of the capital of the Ituri region and that photos of Thomas Kabanga have been put up everywhere."

From a MONUC memo – The United Nations Organization Mission in the Democratic Republic of the Congo
   SECRET
   Subject: Freeing of Thomas Kabanga.
   ICC: "At this time, we are not in a position to ensure the security of ICC personnel in the DRC. All scheduled missions in the country must be cancelled."

I met a former colleague on Herenstraat. He worked on issues in the Kivu region. Mathieu is an idealistic young Frenchman, the son of a Protestant pastor, and a former researcher for Human Rights Watch. He was staggering, and I could see he had been crying. "They're not judges, Claude, they're madmen." I didn't offer to take him for a drink. I took him by the arm and led him back to the Court building.
   "What should we do, Claude? Claus is talking about quitting too."
   "I'm going to Bunia if you want to come along."

30

In the room, Myriam, dressed as if we were going out on the town, was sitting in the armchair, awaiting my return. No, she wasn't worried, she knew I'd be back, and that I had things to do. She asked no questions. I looked at my e-mails. My money was been transferred from Holland and the bank in Kinshasa promised I would be able to draw from my account in Bunia. All the same, I was advised to bring several hundred euros in cash just in case.

Posting from Agence France-Presse: "Thomas Kabanga is expected in Bunia tomorrow after his liberation for procedural reasons by the International Criminal Court. At the Schiphol airport, the militia chief declared that he would resume his political work for a prosperous and autonomous Ituri region. The United Nations forces have reported movement among the population. Inhabitants of Lendu origin appear to be leaving the city."

What am I going to do in that mess?

In the dining room, the waitress spoke only to me. "What will Madame have as an entrée?" Myriam is swathed in her Somali robes. She replied that she'd have the same thing I was having. "I like everything you like." She didn't waste a second on the corpulent Dutch waitress. "Those people don't exist for me anymore."

"What are we going to do in Bunia?"

"We'll see."

"See what?"

"What I can do about Kabanga."

"What can you do?"
"I don't know. But I know I can't just watch."

31

Since she moved in with me, Myriam has stopped wearing Western clothes. Other than that, I know nothing about her.

I looked at the ceiling where the shadows of clouds pierced by the cold moon went scudding past. Myriam was reading Omar Khayyam's poetry. If she doesn't speak, if she hasn't told me about her childhood and her beliefs, it is because she is not ready to, or doesn't completely trust me.

Tomorrow we are leaving for Kinshasa. I have never felt so calm in my life, and I know a little more about the person I will be travelling with. Over these last days, just as we fall asleep, when our breathing comes together like a single person, Myriam began to anticipate the question that would come. She had learned my way of discovering the world, little by little, methodically, with a sort of encyclopedic logic, always step by step. Completely exploring a subject before moving further. She understood that I would not ask her why, when she came to the West, she wanted nothing to do with men's desires. You can't understand how the story ends if you know nothing about its beginning and the detours it took. The beginning of Myriam's story was joyful, even if she was the first child of a father who must have looked on with dismay when he was not presented with a son. In Somalia, girls aren't worth much. But her father had studied medicine in Paris, had gone out with Paris girls, he slept with French women and some of them got better results than he did on the final exams. So Myriam, who was as beautiful as a flower, could pretty much do what she wanted to. After she was born, he had three boys and another girl. Amar, the father, was a revered figure. He treated poor people for free in his office and happily exploited the rich. The vultures that Robin Hood ripped off helped send her to university in the United States and then for an M.A. in international law, which her father considered a source of amusement, since she would be the country's first citizen who had any concept of law. When she returned to Somalia, she began working for Human Rights Watch. The country had turned into a bloodbath. Her father was murdered because he treated the wounded from all clans with no questions asked, and Myriam had, as she put it, "very serious problems." We stopped breathing at the same rhythm, but I knew I couldn't ask the question that logically came next. I turned to her and she slipped the sheet between our bodies. I knew then that she had been raped. Until now, she had said nothing about her past and I'd asked nothing of her. We would be leaving for Kinshasa tomorrow. Nothing is simple with this woman, and the more I lose myself in her, the more I trust her. And the more I fear letting go.

32

Myriam was pretending to sleep. She tried to produce the sound of a woman sleeping so I'd fall asleep and she could think there was still time to say no, and not take the plane, not return to Somalia – she must have considered that. When she closes her eyes, the scenes are tragic, war, certainly, and the triumph of armed stupidity, but most of all it's the twisted mouths, the decayed teeth exposed in laughter, the insults. It's not the rape itself that hurts, it's the contempt and powerlessness. That's why, when we make love, she always says *Gently* and turns her face away. But when she opens her eyes, the shadows on the ceiling are reassuring. A moonbeam lights the room, the trains go by on time, and we can hear the anxious cry of ducks that have lost a duckling in the water lilies in the pool in front of the hotel. A drunk is howling, but those noises comfort her.

"Claude, are you sleeping?"

"No. I was waiting for you to fall asleep."

"Make love to me, gently."

I moved inside her and made myself as light as possible. People don't know anything about lightness and gentleness in bed. For Myriam, the border is so thin between pleasure and horror that a single thrust that is too abrupt brings her back to the place where death began. She knows I'm not raping her. She asked for this penis that labours inside her. She loves my penis that is gentler than all the rest. She believes she loves the man attached to it. At least she trusts him because when she says *Gently*, he slows his rhythm and is sorry for being too eager. That's enough for Myriam to love now: the power to say *Gently* to a man and feel his breathing slow down and his body move to hers instead of looking down on her from his triumphant height, his body an extension of the weapon that tears through flesh. Her flesh is so smooth, like velvet, perfumed and musky, her flesh is like silk, astonishing in its smoothness, and then there is that other flesh inside her, perforated again and again, worked over as if she were a territory to be mined, carved out in secret, bloody caverns. *Gently*, she says.

33

I'm in love with a strange woman who might not love me or might love me for the wrong reasons. Maybe I'm just a passage to another life for her. I wouldn't mind that; at least I'd feel I was accomplishing something, leading someone to another place, a place of peace, a quiet garden. I wouldn't lose anything except a trusting body and an obedient woman. I could get along without Myriam, though when she is here, I feel reassured.

Since her life was more tragic than mine, she has the right to conceal things, and not tell all. I can talk about my ordinary life easily, because that's what it is: ordinary. I have nothing to conceal. My failures in love can be explained, my relationship with women as well, my father's suicide and my mother's accidental death stand like distant events, banal things. They surprised me, but did not hurt me. I search through my past for frustrations, pain, empty spaces so I might enter Myriam's life, and share a sense of torment. But I find nothing except Kabanga and the injustice of him being freed. The last train to Den Haag Central has gone by. It is 2:45 in the morning. Silence will reign until 5:45 when the first train to Utrecht will wake up the crows and the ducks on their pond. Tomorrow evening, we'll be in Kinshasa. This has all happened so quickly, but the mysterious and uncertain future does not worry me. I feel no sense of concern. I am a pearl of salt in the great tide moving toward the coast with the unstoppable logic born of the currents, deep and strong, that determine the climate, throw up and pull down the cliffs, and spend millennia digging out sculptures from the pink granite of Brittany.

I will go where life takes me. Why, all of a sudden, do I feel I am right? Kabanga, three thousand child soldiers, an insolent smile, gold cufflinks, his eyes, not a murderer's but a chief full of himself, grasping for power and wealth through any means possible. A contemptible individual. But I have never lived in the world of primal emotions and I have never considered him as anything other than the accused whom I believe to be guilty. I have left the rigorous universe of justice for the arbitrary and blurred land of passion. I am not so sure that's a good thing, but this is the road I have chosen.

Myriam shifted her weight. I knew she going to speak.

"You want to kill Kabanga?"

I am against capital punishment.

"No."

"You know, it's easy to kill someone. You just need to think he's less human than you are. How long is the flight?"

"Eight hours. We need to sleep."

I couldn't kill, Myriam, I just know I couldn't.

Her breathing grew calm. I followed her rhythm. I couldn't sleep. I thought of Martin, the owner of the wine bar. I never told him I loved him, never told Max, or Tom the Vietnam veteran, or Marco who sells Murano glassware on the Denneweg, or that rotund, puffy-faced man regurgitating his feudal Dutch patois, or Louis, so elegant with his crown of white hair, elegant in thought too, which is no mean feat, or that Norwegian as handsome and frigid as a Viking, or that pair of American lesbians who irritated me to no end, or that old cow who lamented her lost children after the second drink. I thought of all those shipwrecks of solitude who helped me survive, for they were my only human contact. I am leaving them without a word. That's not right. I should have told Martin that I loved him and that he would have been a good father for me. And I should have had enough friendship for Max to tell him he was acting like a teenager. If I ever see them again, I'll tell them. If I ever see them again.

Will I be able to speak and act like a man, and move from cold observation and meticulous analysis to words and actions? I think so, even if I know nothing of the process that appears to be so natural, but is baited with traps, by the illusions of the educated and aware man: the feeling of being superior, the certainty of the analysis, the incomprehension of chance and the unconscious. Only my ignorance of man will keep me from being a man. How many emotions have I repressed that way, abortions of my own self?

34

From Schiphol, I sent an e-mail to Martin, a kind of draft and not very clear, but I believe the meaning was there. It's not easy for a timid heterosexual to write a love letter to a homosexual. I didn't use the word 'love'. I beat around that bush that is 'I love you', used stylistic effects, allusions, evocations, but never the whole sentence. I'll tell him when I come back. I'm not a man yet. I am escaping, still fleeing life. I'll learn. It's not too late.

Gate C 47 at Roissy is a suburb of Kinshasa. Gangs of kids streaked away from their shrieking parents, dignitaries polished their cufflinks, their carry-on bags were larger than my suitcase I'd surrendered to checked baggage, and impatient men harassed the women working the gate. In the fast-food restaurants, families set up camp. Myriam smiled, the undisciplined children amused her, she chatted with the mothers who offered her the cookies they had set aside for their kids. She felt, she told me in the plane, that concupiscent look that said that the White man's Black wife must be good in bed, better than the average Black woman. She also felt the contempt for the woman who has betrayed her people to live with a rich man.

We flew over Paris, headed for Toulouse, turned toward Cairo, and now we are crossing the desert. The man sitting next to me is vaguely a minister, according to his initial introduction, but then come the nuances. He says secretary, assistant, bureau chief. His position varies according to the services he thinks he might be able to render. He greets a man walking past, calling him "esteemed colleague", The children have fallen asleep.

This airplane is a village; almost everyone knows each other. At a thousand euros a ticket, you had to belong to the elite to get a seat, and here is the elite at its best, a little on the corrupt side, wheeling and dealing, incestuous, the Congolese elite at its most typical, straight out of the Mobutu mould. My bureau chief offers to look after my affairs, facilitate my undertakings, to introduce me to everyone, "as a matter of friendship, dear colleague", since I have come to contribute to the development of the Congo. They bled them for all they were worth, as long as they could, those who came to contribute to the development of the country, knowing they too were predators, wild beasts devouring the mines and forests, leaving a few golden turds on the ground riddled with destruction. My new friend gave me three business cards, and he knows the manager of the Memling Hotel where we would be staying. I know that Évangéliste, for that was his name, will show up tomorrow at noon by the pool and exclaim, "Ah, how fortunate it is to run into you, Claude!" He was wearing a Cardin suit from the 1990s and a Rolex on his wrist, and he stank of fragrance for men.

Myriam has a tragic face when she sleeps, long, fine, and delicate like ancient porcelain. A face frozen in time, smooth, as if her features, so pure and free of tension, were those of a dead woman.

What is Kabanga doing tonight in Bunia? Having a quiet supper in the a restaurant, bestowing smiles and handshakes. He is reclaiming his spot. The man is a criminal, but he isn't crazy like some African warlords I had have investigated. He isn't a blood-thirsty killing machine. He earned a diploma in psychology from the Kisangani university. That doesn't qualify him to treat serious afflictions, but he had learned enough from his old dog-eared textbooks, outdated for psychologists everywhere else in the world, to sound convincing when

he talked about the torments of the soul. I knew the man
well. Proud but patient, violent but methodical. Kabanga
wanted to be emperor when he went back to Bunia. Like
Napoleon, he was exiled, then returned. But Kabanga is
no Bonaparte. He is a man of meagre personal
ambitions, which makes him a prudent specimen. He
wouldn't want to frighten the Kinshasa government with
a triumphant return. He will lie low, like a patient croco-
dile with one eye open, motionless in the muddy water,
waiting. Then he will swim toward the bank and –
clack! – devour the nearest child playing by the water,
and then its mother and the rest of its family if necessary.

The passenger next to me asked me what I thought of
the situation in the Congo. I told him I didn't really know
his country. You know that Kabanga has returned home?
I don't know any Kabanga. He launched into the story
of the poor patriot perverted by foreign powers, a good
man who made mistakes, but everyone makes mistakes
in this country. What are mistakes anyway? Fighting,
warfare, and crimes, but who hasn't committed crimes in
this country? "He's a good man. He has style. He has
assurance and he talks well. You can see he's an intellectual. And he's intelligent. My cousin lives in Bunia and
he told me about the way he came back. He didn't allow
the members of his party to come and celebrate at the
airport for fear of opening old wounds. He just wants to
be an ordinary citizen again, ready to cooperate in the
development of his country and the stability of the Ituri
region."

What about the three thousand child soldiers? The
bureau chief, or whoever he was, told me those were
White man's stories, you never know the age of a child,
and anyway, children like to fight and play with guns. I
think of my child soldiers, Josué, Béatrice, and the other
witnesses, Marie and Aristide who lost the protection of
the Court and are wandering the hills or the suburbs of

Bunia, hiding, because rumour says that Kabanga has decided to kill his accusers. He's just waiting for the right time. I know him, my Kabanga, he's a patient man. I am too. I need to learn the African way of doing things. The African way, five hundred doses of tritherapy.

I looked at my neighbour's wrist.

"How much is that Rolex?"

"Three thousand euros. It's one of the least expensive and I got it through a friend."

"The civil service must pay well in the Democratic Republic of the Congo."

"No, not at all. I have some money from the family."

"What did the family do under Mobutu?"

That's not the African way. I need to learn to ask questions without asking them, because my neighbour suddenly goes to sleep. This world is not for me. The family must have been in diamonds, gold mines, in the obligatory taxes levied on unfortunate foreigners, they must have been attentive to orders, delivering up a cousin when the authorities demanded it. I don't know, I'm imagining. To wear a Rolex and travel first class, and dress like a scarecrow from the 1990s, you had to be a bandit or the son of one. But in this airplane, a bandit isn't a criminal. He's a minister or a public servant.

The bureau chief woke me up. "Kinshasa." I asked him if he could find me a Rolex for the same price. He smiled. Myriam was sleeping with her fists clenched, like a child. We were landing; I felt the deceleration and the pressure blocking my ears. He wanted to meet to see whether he could help me with my plans and enterprises. This is the first time in my life I have had no project. I have only a destination: a strange city and a companion who is still clenching her fists. How could I explain to this man who is used to skimming off a piece of everything that passes, and starting quick friendships with anyone who might be useful to him, and dropping those who turn out not to be, that this isn't "how men live?" The bureau chief will drop by the Memling to talk about the Rolex and my future plans. Joseph, whom I had already met in The Hague, was waiting for us on the tarmac. He took our passports and led us into the VIP salon, then disappeared to take care of the formalities. In Kinshasa, half an Airbus 340 ended up in the VIP salon while several dozen Josephs took care of the formalities. The bureau chiefs paraded their power, since all of them had been enemies at one time, ministers wandered past, glancing around to see whether a journalist wasn't waiting for them, ambassadors from lesser countries cooled their heels, girls were on the lookout for customers fresh off the boat. Myriam found a spot between two leather couches. She dug herself in like a fearful animal in a makeshift lair. She seemed so gentle and fragile in this salon full of ogres and predators. The bureau chief smiled and nodded in my direction. Joseph returned with our passports in his hand like a pair of trophies.

Joseph is not the brightest light going. He has a diploma from Kisangani university like Kabanga, but he specialized in communications. For the past three years he has worked for the clerk of the Court in Kinshasa, and his job is to explain the ICC's legal decisions to the local media. Colleagues have told me that during press conferences, he stumbles and grasps for words, gets tripped up in the "directives" handed down by The Hague, and inevitably ends by declaring that justice will be just because it is international. The journalists in the capital considered him a mercenary, a fake. Yet there was no one more honest than Joseph.

He piloted his Cherokee through the night, along the road to the centre of town. They call it the Highway. Vehicles move like ships through the reddish mist, hundreds of ghosts, zombies, shades, and spectres wander in this fog of sand and dust, illuminated by headlights and cooking fires where women sat, selling a few onions or bananas and or some manioc. Men weighted down with burdens slipped among the vehicles. This isn't a highway, it is an anthill, and no horn can frighten the ants. They challenge the four-wheeled monsters, blocking their way and their shiny metal, casting contemptuous looks at them when they finally decide to let the highway do its job. The disorder delighted me, the warm breezes excited me, and I loved the way the dust danced and scrolled like red smoke. Everything was completely foreign, it corresponded to nothing I knew, and I wondered why I had waited so long – why I had waited so long for life. Because here it is, Life, this teeming unpredictability, non-stop improvisation, a carnival ride gone mad, a provincial circus trotting out three Spanish hens, two camels, and a gnu. Life in its smallest detail, at the level everyone lives. Waking up on an uncertain morning, with the sound of children, a glance outside to see if the sky is grey or in flames. I have never lived that way.

Before we got to the hotel, Joseph confided his apprehensions. Ever since the rumours brought the news that Kabanga would be freed, his men have been preparing his revenge. Houses have been burned. Weapons hidden under the woodpile or in false ceilings have reappeared on the streets. The old uniforms too, ones from Rwanda. "Back to the future." Two witnesses were decapitated and their bodies dumped in front of the Lebanese restaurant, on avenue de la Libération. He feared others would meet the same fate. It is impossible to remain anonymous when rumours make the law.

The lobby of the Memling: lacquered wood, valets in livery, VIP reception, credit cards, Dior suits, and Rolex watches contrast with life. Dinner by the pool, Chinese men trading entire mines for a promise of credit,

American dollars for everything, even a bottle of Perrier. Here is the official Africa, that of ministers and top civil servants. I pictured Charles Taylor on the stand in The Hague, the prosperous businessman, his look of contempt and apparent disinterest in his own trial. These people live outside of their world. Maybe Kabanga, the psychologist, could explain how a man becomes a predator, how he comes to devour his brothers and sisters, a lying sorcerer, a professional imposter, a wheeler-dealer and murderer and torturer, while displaying a smile for foreigners from the World Bank or the representative of Chinese investors.

Myriam veiled herself in luminous yellow. She ordered a Coke. Her clothing made her all the more desirable. The veil underlined her delicate features that hinted at the promise of her concealed body. A man looked at her eyes and imagined her legs, her sculpted nose and breasts. The veil conceals and invites desire. More than Western clothes that advertise the merchandise, the veil provokes violent desire. The veil demands to be torn away despite the prudery and dissimulation. Is that why Islam has so often insisted on veiling women – to provoke concupiscence and mad desire?

I didn't tear away her veil, but I did pull it off abruptly. I forgot my old hesitations and pushed Myriam onto the bed without a word. No kisses, no caresses, just the ragged breathing of sexual desire, the rough, staccato movements of possession, the heavy grunting of masculine satisfaction. She moaned in protest, then told me drily, "That's the way they used to do it to me." Another part of life I haven't understood. I won't tell her it's the veil's fault. I won't tell her that I'm not a rapist. I was carried away by desire. It's become all too clear to me that I don't know how to love.

35

The Democratic Republic of the Congo is a tax bureau that follows the public-private partnership model. The private sector is the government, which is also public. The underclasses traffic in cigarettes and chewing gum, toothpaste and Kleenex. The policeman taxes the poor guy he picks out of a traffic jam and who isn't wearing his seatbelt. The mining official never lets anyone consult a geological survey without demanding a week's worth of food if he's honest, and a house if he's moved from poverty to proactive corruption. The pawn in the elevator whispers that he can take care of certain introductions. The bureau chief's secretary would love to have dinner with you, and her boss demands part of your enterprise. But here is the dilemma: I am going to set up shop in Bunia, and but don't know if I'll go into gold, diamonds, the restaurant business, or simply fritter away my savings. I know one thing for sure, which I cannot say to them: I want to observe Kabanga and study the consequences of his liberation for the city and the region. Joseph has already alluded to the mysterious disappearance of witnesses and victims. I am a kind of spy for my own justice system, and I know that a spy needs a good cover. The Minister of Justice, with whom I conversed on the phone and by e-mail when I was at The Hague, and who was responsible for Kabanga being arrested, will help me settle in Bunia. Afterward, he says, if I strike it rich in diamonds or gold or something else, we'll talk. He smiles, satisfied with himself, knowing that I have seen the sword of Damocles he has just hung over my head. He is waiting for me, and I won't escape. He wrote a note for the Minister of the Interior. I will receive a residence permit for one year and the police and local administration in Bunia will be instructed to leave me alone. To do things right, unlike my earlier mission to the Ivory Coast, I invited him and his wife to have dinner at the Memling. He looked at his schedule and, surprise, he was free this evening, something that rarely occurs.

The dinner was ceremonial to a fault, not poolside as I had reserved, but in the dining room. Since when do you drink champagne with snails and lamb shanks? I don't know, but the Minister and his wife shovelled it in. A bottle of old Armagnac topped it off. Myriam dozed to the sound of Madame's comments about fabric and clothing, mostly Dior. She wears traditional African styles for official soirées such as tonight, but otherwise her threads come from Paris. "My clothes come from my house," Myriam said, but no one heard.

36

"What are we going to do in Bunia?" Myriam asked.

"I don't know. I really don't. We'll see and I'll decide."

"And what will I do in Bunia while you see and decide?"

"You'll help me."

37

Myriam has taken over our room at the Hotel Memling. She bought flowers and a vase to put them in. She got her hands on two folk-art paintings that so-called painters were selling off in front of the hotel. A pastiche of Tintin, *The Adventures of Claude in the Congo*, and an awkward but touching baobab tree casting its benevolent shadow over a stunted child, protecting it from the murderous sun. On the bed, she set out tropical clothing made of linen, and several cotton shirts of remarkable quality.

"Try them on?"

I didn't want to. I've never cared about clothes. A pair of jeans and some wrinkled shirts suit me fine. And I don't like looking at myself; I don't like myself physically. "Go ahead." At first I wouldn't co-operate. This kind of dress-up was ridiculous. Then I put on a pair of white écru pants whose fabric was like a caress against my legs, and a loose, ochre-coloured shirt that floated like a fine delicate veil around my body. The cloth was light and soft. I ventured a look in the mirror. I wasn't so ugly, after all. I was even a little elegant, and I rejoiced in that elegance. Myriam was offering me another image of myself, the one she wanted to see, perhaps. I should have always dressed like that. She laughed. I smiled at my own awkward words. "You see, it's simple." At that moment I knew I loved her, not for the pleasure of being dressed by her, but for the man she suspected was inside me, the one she was inventing. If she dies or leaves me, I'll continue dressing this way, because it suits me and makes me less ugly.

The telephone rang. It was Joseph, and it was urgent. He was nervous and worried. I met him in the lobby. He led me outside where we were immediately mobbed by vendors selling Tintin paintings, Marlboros and matches, and cards for mobile phones. The air was heavy, you could feel the storm that would soon break and drive these people toward the nearest makeshift shelter. Six or seven of them surrounded us as we were trying to walk. Joseph pulled out a pistol and fired into the air. I was more frightened than the vendors. They were used to gunshots, and they retreated quietly.

"You're armed!"

"You should be too," he told me as if I was dimmest idiot on earth. "One of the child soldiers, Josué, his parents just got kidnapped by Kabanga's men. They're holding them hostage in Bunia. They won't release them unless the kid gives himself up."

"Where's the kid?"

"Here, in Kinshasa."

"Can you find him?"

"I think so."

I wanted to go back to Myriam, go back in time fifteen minutes, to that moment when I felt the joy of being a woman's creation.

She was sleeping deeply, taking long, peaceful breaths. She hugged a pillow in her arms like a child. I lay down close to her and kissed the back of her neck. "I'm sleeping," she muttered. At least that's what I understood. "I love you," I answered. I said it, and she heard me. Now I could concentrate on my work. But maybe I lied, because the sound of those three words has made me dream ever since.

38

Here, money trumps everything else. The smell of it wipes away principles, eliminates barriers, and sidesteps laws. Here, small change for the White man is a fortune for the Black. Historically, White men have understood this, and even today, they use that imbalance, sometimes without realizing it. And yet sometimes, it can be very useful.

The sun exploded into the room. Myriam was making coffee. Joseph phoned. He found Josué, and was with him. I took a shower and left without drinking any coffee. She kissed me. Apparently, she did hear my profession of love. I was happy and a little wound up, I hadn't slept much and spent my time analysing. I weighed the pros and the cons, and believed I was right. In this country, money smells sweeter than revenge. Kabanga knew there were dozens of witnesses who had accused him, one more, one less, it's all the same to him, but if he could make some profit off them, he would. I know the man. And God did I despise him! Ideas don't motivate him, and he was following no political plan. He would accept ransom for Josué's parents. And I would pay it.

The meeting makes me anxious. Josué isn't a child anymore, he is nineteen. I know he had no childhood. I'd had a child's childhood, and he had an adult's. At thirteen, he had already killed a man. At that age, in disbelief I discovered death existed thanks to the TV, then I studied it in dictionaries and books. He knew the smell of rotting bodies, and the victim's coagulated blood on his basketball shorts – because blood shoots out like a fountain when you slash a man's throat with a machete – the death rattle, the lost look of someone who feels nothingness taking over. I knew nothing about that. All I knew about death was images and representations. It's like Bunia: I know everything, but understand nothing.

Josué paced in circles around the room. He was already a handsome man, or would be one soon. He spoke very little about his pain. As soon as he felt danger, he stiffened. You could feel him ready to attack. He talked about his rap group, almost singing the words he used. He wanted to find a cassette to prove to us that he has talent. He's positive he does. Self-assured and fragile, in equal measure. More self-assured than I was. Josué is a born leader. I know, because I'd read everything about him. I knew that at age six, he fought with his parents for the right to go to school. He refused to be poor the way they were. At school he was the head of his class. He excelled at soccer, and at ten, he started a rap group that took its inspiration from *zouk* music. At twelve, still head of his class and the top goal scorer on his team, he recorded a cassette and sold it in the marketplace. He had a remarkable sense of organization. A few weeks before he was kidnapped by Kabanga, his rap group started putting on shows in restaurants and bars in Bunia. He was thirteen years old.

"We'll protect you, Josué, and we'll find your parents. I know what you went through, I read your testimony for the Court, you and Kabanga's other child soldiers."

"I'm not the other child soldiers. I'm Josué, and you know nothing about my nightmares. The kind of sweat you have from a nightmare – do you know what that's like? It smells bad, it smells like bodies rotting in the swamp. When I wake up, I stink like a corpse. I *am* a corpse."

"We're going to take care of you, Josué."

"I'm not sick, sir, I've had a spell cast on me. The evil spirit lives inside me."

The conversation wasn't going anywhere.

I told him about my plan to free his parents. It wasn't really a plan, it was an intuition, a theory, the kind I'm always producing. I construct reality from data, and when I hit it, I hope it will fit into the way I imagined it.

He was afraid to see his parents again. "Do you love your parents?" He froze and stared me down as if I'd insulted him.

There, now I know, that's a question you never ask a child, even if he's nearly twenty years old and, since the war started six years ago, he has lived the life of an adult. In this place, a child can't say he doesn't love his parents.

"You know everything, but you understand nothing. You talk to me like I was a kid. Take a look at this kid."

He pulled off his Lakers t-shirt and slipped down his jogging pants that were too big for him, then dropped his underpants to the floor.

"Look. They cut off one of my balls when I was fourteen because I wouldn't rape a girl I knew. 'You're impotent,' the chief told me, 'you don't need both your balls.' The scar on my arm, that's from a machete, and the black spot on my shoulder, that's a stray bullet, and I won't tell you what the chiefs did to my ass for fun when they were drunk. Do you know the pain when someone sticks a lit cigar in your ass? Kabanga loved Cuban cigars."

He got dressed calmly and sat on the gold-coloured couch decorated with mismatched cushions. He looked at me and waited. He was a mongoose, and maybe I was the snake.

"Do you want me to take you to a doctor?"

"My wounds are healed. But the wounds in my head – you know about those? You, you can sleep. And when you sleep, in your head do you see bloody faces, women's parts staved in by sledgehammers, when you sleep, do you hear the rattling of dying animals, and when you look at them with their bellies slit open, do you see the faces you saw at the market? When you sleep, what do you see? I want to go back in time. I want to be thirteen even if I'm nineteen. Can you do that for me? Take me back?"

I know very well I can't. Every study I've read has pointed out that the vast majority of child soldiers are forever rejected by the stream of normal life. They never manage to return to childhood, they move through life like a no-man's-land. Never a child, never an adult. The past has been stolen, and the future forbidden.

"If you came to Bunia with us, with my wife and me, maybe we could help you find some sort of justice."

As I spoke those words, I realized, without thinking, that I have taken on responsibility for a nineteen-year-old child. A child who will end up on the edges of society or, worse, again become a child who kills because that is all he knows. I was offering to adopt a potential psychopath.

Josué accepted my offer. I would protect him and help free his parents. He wasn't so sure they will want to see him again because they are ashamed of him, but he accepted all the same.

39

I returned to the hotel, and Myriam listened attentively to my explanations, and my plan for Josué. She smiled as I struggled to think it through.

"Is he likeable? Were you moved by him? Did you ask him what he wanted? Do you want to adopt him?"

"Myriam, I want to free the parents of a child soldier, not open an adoption agency!"

She sat up in the bed. Her diamond gaze could slice through glass. "What did you come here for?" I avoided her shining eyes, and looked away from her naked body. Feelings make for untrustworthy counsel – so says the wisdom of the ages. I lay down and tried to ignore her graceful body that moved close to mine. She slipped a leg between my legs and wrapped one arm around my shoulder.

How was I going to organize the operation to free Josué's parents? In my initial wave of anger and shame when the Court betrayed justice in the name of legal procedure, I thought I would move to Bunia as a sort of spy for justice, real justice, and observe the tragic consequences of Kabanga being freed. I would make a report the way I used to in my former job as analyst, I would alert the NGOs and my ex-colleagues from the Court, and maybe my report would heap shame on men obsessed with procedure and idealized law. Now I had to act, I needed a plan. I am not a man of action; I understood that much during my few youthful adventures as a militant. When life takes hold of me in its concrete grasp, I lose all strength, my power of analysis deserts me, and I become the emotional adolescent I do not want to be.

I have to be wary of emotion. And Myriam is an emotion. At the same time, I feel that my body and other repressed flaws and hollows within me are drawn to her by threads I can't name. I feel them sticking to my skin like spider webs. I tried, gently, to pull away from her warmth as she pressed against me.

Tomorrow, Josué will join us at the hotel, and we will plan our stay in Bunia. Myriam is breathing softly on my neck. Making love now would seal a covenant that would be definitive, or almost. I needed to reflect, step back from life and its emotions. When I have accomplished my work, whose nature I don't even know, then I can let myself explore the misty, mysterious territory that lies beyond reason. But not before.

40

1) After Josué, find the others, the men and women who testified or were scheduled to and who have lost the protection of the Court.
2) Bring them together and invent a new form of protection. How?
3) For the children, this excludes a return to their families. In any case, the families generally reject child soldiers. How to do this without the families?
4) Establish myself in Bunia, fit in, play a role, maybe buy a business, find allies. Not very simple.
5) Who controls the city? Kabanga or the Lebanese traders in gold and diamonds? The Lebanese mafia? Are the Ugandans still there? And the Rwandans?
6) Become 'African'.

When I got to 7, I put down my pen, looked at myself in the mirror, and realized the man I saw did not know where he was headed.

41

Morning in Kinshasa. By nine o'clock, the street vendors are already hungry. They woke up at five. They walked several kilometres with their meagre merchandise perched on their heads. Their bellies are empty and their eyes are empty. Impatiently they wait for government employees and NGO and UN workers to purchase a pack of Marlboros, which will give them enough to buy a few fritters and calm the complaining of their empty stomachs that you can actually hear out loud. I admire their resilience. So much hunger and poverty, and so little anger and envy in their eyes. I buy cigarettes even if I don't smoke, and Dentyne Ice gum even if I don't chew it. I buy fruit juice, wondering if it will give me the runs. I don't give to beggars, but I do to vendors. I play the game of work for pay. I always pick up my change. I pay the fair price, the White price, of course. But it's fairer than fair. It seems there are more car horns here than in Montreal or Paris, and as many traffic lights, but they don't work. A sort of imitation modernity, an ersatz of Western society and its wealth. Meanwhile, we inhabit an exuberant urban jungle. To my surprise, I feel quite at home in this perpetual excitement, the excessive shouting and laughter. Why does this disorderly life please me, while I fear the slightest tremble that Myriam sets off in my mind and body? I must like disorder that comes from the outside. I'll have to resolve that contradiction; my answer is not convincing. But later. Right now I have to talk to Josué.

42

Myriam adored Josué and the feeling was mutual. "I always wanted to have a child, but I never trusted fathers." He watched the water flow into the bathtub, played with the faucets, accidentally turned on the shower and the spray of water frightened him like a kitten. He asked what the bidet was for. He was just shy of nineteen, but suddenly he was seven years old again and discovering how a bathtub and a shower worked. He was seven or ten again when he let Myriam wash him. In spite of his timid smile when he stepped out of the bathroom, his eyes were older than mine, as if this child had aged faster than I have.

Now, Josué was sleeping in the next room. Myriam, I imagined, was pretending to sleep.

The door opened. Josué said, "I'm afraid, there are spirits, I don't want to sleep alone. I'm afraid." He was shaking, sweating, terrorized, with staring eyes he looked at the ceiling, the walls, and all the objects that might turn into monsters and ghosts. "Come and sleep with me." Myriam's voice was like a caring mother. Josué lay down shyly by her side. She took him in her arms like the child he had become for a moment. Tomorrow, I know, he could kill. I would sleep on the sofa. And Myriam was sleeping with Josué who was also a man.

43

I saw Bunia from the sky, dazzled by the sun bouncing off the blue tents of the refugees and displaced persons scattered over the hills. The Tupolev, its engine coughing, made a low-altitude fly-by of the city. In his South African accent, the pilot said, "Welcome to Bunia" over the scratchy PA system. Bunia is just a main street in the centre of a spider web that weaves its threads out to infinity. Josué pointed to a hill. That was where he lived. No huts, no houses, just endless blue canvas. "It's pretty with the hills around the town," Myriam said. I was wrong; there is no airport in Bunia, just a dirt landing strip with prefabs and white metal containers branded with MONUC letters and the blue UN logo. Terrorized by the plane's squealing metal, Josué grabbed my arm and held on for dear life during the final approach. The landing was brutal. Josué dug his nails into my arm and turned to at me as if the plane was going to fall to pieces around us, and I would be his saviour, his last resort. Such terror in his eyes, and such letting go as his head fell upon my shoulder and his body slipped closer to mine. I put an unsure hand on his, and he squeezed mine as if it were a life preserver. I turned and looked him in the eye. "Don't be afraid, I'm here." Then I took him in my arms. His body was hot, he stank of the sweat of fear, and choked back his tears when the plane slowed on the bumpy strip full of holes, then taxied with a more gentle rhythm until our progress was like an African trail that he knows the feel of. He pulled his nails out of my flesh, but did not leave my arms. He started breathing again, relaxed a little, and raised his head. "Now I won't be afraid of planes anymore."

44

Joseph was travelling with us to Bunia, and he had taken care of everything. A Jeep Cherokee was waiting for us, and with it, government employees proposing their services to help facilitate our undertakings. Joseph is the last honest Congolese. He believes in principles, justice, democracy, and honesty, but he looked more preoccupied with survival management, and asked me for a few American dollars to distribute to worthy hands. Josué was nervous, Myriam, ravishing. Bunia's main street unfolded like a movie set. An old Western, with businesses like saloons, storefronts painted with blue stripes at the bottom, and gabled roofs above where snipers could hide like in the pictures and war comics. The Hôtel Bunia sat facing a trading post: 'We Buy Diamonds'. Iron bars, muscled, well-armed men. Here was the reign of armed force and everything that could be traded; law is the law of 'no law'. There were a lot of Whites in the lobby, Lebanese most of them, sipping tea and telling their amber beads. A few girls were already sitting at the bar, sucking on a Coke and broadcasting their boredom. Josué kept turning around and grabbing my arm. "I know that one, that guy there." He pushed me toward the wall and pointed his trembling finger at a chubby, stubbly Lebanese man. "After the fighting, he did business with the Rwandans, and Kabanga sold him all his diamonds and all his gold."

Josué wanted to sleep with us. When we talked, sometimes he took my hand, and that put me ill at ease.

The concept of adjoining rooms doesn't exist here, but there was a suite with three beds, cracked walls, ill-fitting windows, a dysfunctional shower, pretty little green lizards, a lightbulb that did more blinking than illuminating, photos of gorillas on the walls, and an air conditioner that huffed and puffed like an overworked draft horse. I wasn't wrong this time. For reasons not explained, the restaurant menu tended toward Asian food, and included Vietnamese cheese. I felt strangely reassured. Some things I got right. The owner sat down at our table with a bottle of Côtes du Rhône that had spent ten years heating up on the shelf. Yes, I'm here to do business, as the saying goes. Sayed was Kurdish. He wore a fighter's moustache and had eyes like a cat.

Josué whispered that he was going to look for the other witnesses, and would be back with news. He slipped away. I didn't ask questions about Kabanga; I would wait until he came to me. Sayed talked business. He was looking for an associate, told me about the cut he took on the girls, who happened to be the best ones in town, and the low cost of Vietnamese imports. Josué didn't return, and I was worried. Myriam kept her veil on, but didn't say no to the wine. She got up and started dancing to a Céline Dion song playing on the radio: *Tu ne m'as pas regardée danser*. I felt responsible for Josué, not like a father, but as a legal guardian. Maybe I had failed in both my responsibilities, and worse, I had no idea what to do tomorrow. The feeling was intolerable, as if life was wheeling out of control. Everything in my world was planned and organized, and yes, I admired Myriam who was dancing, but I closed my eyes. I went up to the room with the excuse that I had phone calls to make. A lizard was sleeping on my notebook. I lay down without turning off the light that was flashing as if it had a terminal case of hiccups. Myriam came in, tipsy, and wanted to make love. I pushed her away, and told her coldly that I was worried because Josué hadn't come back. His absence was a good thing, she pointed out, because we could love each other now. I don't love her, at least not this evening. Her affection was a distraction. I was thinking about Josué and what I would need to do tomorrow.

At a loss, I fell asleep after three hours with my face buried in my notebook, and the lizard looking at me and wondering what I was doing. Maybe it was the same lizard that had moved in on my worktable. My program for the next day was simple: get up, take a shower, eat, wait for Josué, and an idea that might come or something that might happen. Myriam was snoring softly, another irritation.

45

No hot water today. I hate being cold. No eggs either. Someone forgot to deliver them. The boss expressed his regrets. He proposed Vietnamese cheese and a warm Primus because the refrigerator went off when the generator stopped. He could make me a cold Nescafé if I didn't want to drink beer. "It's on the house." Myriam thought it was amusing since she had known much worse, but I was so irritated I surprised myself. I obviously had a long way to go before becoming African. No news from Josué. I went back to the room with a cold Nescafé. The lizard was waiting on the little table, and he seemed to be mocking me. In this unfinished universe, I was like a lost boat drifting on the current, lifted and tipped by mighty swells. Shipwrecked in Bunia.

I wanted to go home. What a ridiculous thought! Home has become the place where I settle temporarily. I imagined the word as I waited for the boss to tell me whether we could eat. Home could have been a room decorated with a favourite painting, a library full of books with words to guide me, a house with children, a neighbourhood with neighbours and merchants who sometimes get on my nerves, a city filled with strangers whose habits I know, but also a few friends I loved, whose faults are appreciated as much as their qualities. Home could be a park, a sidewalk, a woman, a forest. Yes, a woman like a dark forest into which one ventures carefully, but I knew it couldn't be Myriam because I took her the way you choose a vacation destination, with excitement and emotion, of course, and affection too, but I was using her like a hotel room or a highway. I would always be somewhere else. So I waited. I had no other choice. Josué was still missing and that worried me.

46

Today we were going to eat chicken and noodles. The generator went back to work. The beer was still warm. Myriam left to buy fabric. The chubby Lebanese was sweating profusely, and when he sat down at my table without introducing himself, I choked back a wave of nausea. "Karim," he said, and offered a damp hand. "Claude," I reciprocated.

"So you've come to Bunia to do business."

"Yes, I'm considering the possibilities."

"Maybe I can help you. Mostly I'm in diamonds, but pretty soon things will be opening up in gold and coltan. We need friends and extra cash."

"We?"

"Friends, important people, politicians who want to give new life to the local economy."

"I don't know anything about Ituri. Who do you mean, what group are you talking about?"

"I'll be speaking to you, Claude, when the time comes."

I knew very well whom he was talking about. Joseph got me the latest MONUC reports. Since his return, Kabanga has chosen the way of discretion, but the Hema merchants who had always dominated the city's economy were meeting in his villa. That was the same group that took power in 2002, pillaged the gold mines, trafficked in diamonds, and controlled the coltan market.

"Mister, Mister..."

A little, frizzy-haired, red-headed boy was pulling on my sleeve. Ten years old, maybe, black skin and black eyes that stared up at me. He asked me if he could have some chicken please, Mister. I ordered chicken and noodles and he swallowed them down. He gave me a scrap of paper and I read it. "Hi boss, forget my parents. They don't want me. They weren't kidnapped. They wanted money. I found Marie, Aristide, Béatrice too and other child soldiers. We have guns. We are training to make justice. You will be proud of us. We're like you, we want justice. When we're ready, I'll send you another message."

Benjamin, since that was his name, told me, as his mouth overflowed with noodles, that I had to answer. In spite of the overwhelming heat, I felt cold shivers. I was shaking. Stumbling over the words, as if for the first time in my life writing was an obstacle course, a hundred-metre hurdle, I tried to compose.

"Josué, justice isn't revenge. Justice is what's fair and proven [I'm writing stupidities, he won't understand any of this]. Take the time to think about it. Murdering a murderer isn't justice [again, I'm sure he won't understand]. Don't do anything until we talk. Justice must be just."

But I'm here because justice wasn't just.

"Where's Josué?"

"I don't know any Josué."

Benjamin wanted a beer before he left. I ordered him one.

Myriam returned, disappointed. The market didn't have much to offer.

She wasn't as upset as I was by Josué's letter. In fact, she wasn't upset at all.

"Is Kabanga guilty?"

"Yes, according to the proof we had."

"So what's the problem?"

"Here, I know, there is no problem. Josué and the rest of them know, in their flesh and their souls, that Kabanga is guilty. But revenge, even when it's justified, isn't justice. There is the rule of law."

"We left the Court because the rule of law prevented justice being done, Claude."

Ever since I left The Hague, I have wondered how I would react when I came face to face with Kabanga. You have to understand. The man was my intimate enemy. I spent three years of my life noting down and explaining and describing his vices, his turpitude, and his crimes. Let's just say that my hatred was reasonable and well documented.

Then, suddenly, he walked into the restaurant, and he seemed as normal as I was, imposing and handsome like in the photos, wearing a white écru linen jacket. Lately he had become a pastor, and he was sporting an enormous cross, the kind the Pope wears on his chasuble. I felt nothing, only curiosity. Was I incapable of emotion? The man I had been hunting for three years was shaking hands with the crowd like a candidate running for office, with dignity and elegance. Everyone greeted him with respect.

He introduced himself. "I am Thomas Kabanga, pastor of the Evangelical Church of Bunia. May I?" I said nothing. He sat down and ordered rice and beans. His two bodyguards took a table next to ours. The pastor needed tight security. We ate in silence and I wondered what kind of mess I'd gotten myself into. There I was, breaking bread with Kabanga.

"Some friends have told me you're Canadian. What a big, beautiful country. Those same friends also told me you wish to invest in Bunia. That is surprising. Here, only oil and mining companies from Canada dare to tread. Your wife is a beauty."

Myriam lowered her eyes.

"Mr. Canadian, I am the protector and pastor of

Bunia. I preach the word of God and I protect the people of my community. In the past I was forced to use violence, but I believe that time has passed. As my friend Karim told you, we need support to better develop our region. We would be happy to have you among us. If ever you need advice, I am at your service."

He rose. His hand cut through the air in front of me; that might have been his blessing. He offered his hand. I hesitated, then shook it.

47

Plouézec, I need your spring tides and morning mists and the sun that breaks through without warning. That place could be my home. To leave, with no preparation – that is my only wish. I have just shaken the hand of my worst enemy. Obviously he knew who I was, and he couldn't care less. There is nothing here but jostle and uproar, pugnacious, demanding odours, sweat and dime-store perfume, a concert of car horns and shouting, harsh colours, tragicomedy, theatre, and representation. I love this cacophony, the sheer disorder of it, I'd like to slip into it like a skin, but I can't. A thread is holding me back and I don't know which one it is.

Wherever you look, the sea is missing. It seems as distant as happiness, that honey I've never tasted. Only sounds and the rustling of the earth, only human noise and brutal cacophony reach my ears. Those things attract and repel me. A spring tide, the kind that washes the bed of the bay and tears down the cliffs, that would do me a world of good. A little peace, a little silence. No such luck. Myriam has started lecturing me on justice and right, equity and vengeance. I think of Josué and my other children that I don't know. On my left wrist is the scar inflicted by his fear when the plane landed. My children! Now I'm inventing children for myself. I don't even know them. They're paper children, testimony children, like dolls. I thought I knew everything about their pain. But only their wounds I've never seen and the thousands of pages of words I've never heard bind me to them. Reading life doesn't mean you understand it, it's only constructing, deducing, and imagining. You can read the world, but not a human being. I don't know them. I've never experienced the first hesitations, then the screams, the first steps, and then the first wound. I'm eager to defend them, but can I love them? What if I didn't love them? What if they were all Kabangas waiting to spring? No need to love them to defend them. Besides, how can I defend them? I can't do anything for them, I'm not with the Court anymore, I can only support them, give them a little money, try and give them advice. I remember a study written by an American psychologist. "We cannot transform a child into an adult with impunity. By imposing adult behaviour on children, we deprive them of their childhood rites. When they torture and kill, they do it with a child's eyes and reflexes. When they become adults, they have a child's night-mares, not an adult's. They carry their stolen childhood into their adult lives. This creates a child adult, a schizo-phrenic individual who suffers from the violence inflicted, but knows only violence as a way of self-expression." My paper children are sick. I need to think. In this forsaken place, I am doing what all expatriates do when they try to think or forget: I drink. I don't even know why, as if drinking were a form of breathing, something automatic, a conditioned response.

48

I have had no news of Josué for ten days. Myriam disappeared on a regular basis, then came back to tell me about her meetings with the League of Women for Peace. Karim insisted that we do business together, and he stank as badly as ever. Madeleine, a prostitute, sat with me sometimes and told me she liked me and how she was willing to do it for free with me. The lizard kept an eye on me. The White UN workers avoided me, I didn't know why. Yes, I did know, and I was not saddened. As if it were in the order of things, the order of my life. Stay in the margins like a note, an observation next to a page that others have written, and that frightens me, because if I begin to write there too, the words running with blood and emotion will paralyse me and I'll suffocate. Give nothing of yourself, and don't let go. I prefer to comment on life as I observe it. The lizard doesn't believe me. The Primus is warm, the noodles are cold, the Vietnamese cheese comes from the last century. I should try and find some satisfaction in those things, but I can't. I should make Sayed an offer: I'll take over management of his restaurant and turn it into a French bistro. When I make an effort, I can cook reasonably well.

Sayed stopped by. I asked him to sit down, poured him some Primus, and told him about my idea for the bistro. He smiled. I understood that the cheese was Vietnamese and the cuisine vaguely Asian because his wife was Vietnamese. For a Kurd to be married to a woman from Vietnam, and running a hotel in Bunia, did not particularly surprise me. There are waves of migration, exile, and conflict. If you spend time analysing the world's uproar, classifying and understanding the succession of waves, everything finds its explanation and becomes normal. But what about the encounter of two individuals, a union born, perhaps, of two sets of tragedies? "It's the first time you've asked me a personal question." Sayed lowered his eyes, as if to reflect a moment, then his face brightened. The story began on a beach, a chance meeting on the sand. This beach wasn't at rest, waiting for the spring tides. This one, a Spanish one on the Canary Islands, was punished by a storm that had capsized trawlers, tuna boats, and improvised craft loaded with illegals fleeing the conflicts of Asia and Africa. That night there were more than two hundred human castaways, including Sayed, fleeing Kurdistan. Fifteen years earlier, a seven-year-old Vietnamese girl was taken on by a French ship, dropped in a boat people camp in Malaysia, and then accepted as a refugee in Spain. To show her gratitude, she became a Red Cross volunteer, then an employee. They offered her the Canaries with their sandy beaches. She loved the sea until it started sending her corpses and refugees with nothing but the clothes on their back. The night of the storm, she discovered a single survivor: Sayed. She decided to care for him. He lowered his eyes, raised them again, and smiled. "You know the rest of the story." No, I didn't. Of course I could imagine it and construct it by myself, without hearing it and its experience first-hand. But I wanted to know the rest, the first kiss, the first night, the thrill of it, the look in the eye, the words, the silences, the rustling of the sheets, the colour of the room, the birdsong and the calls in the street outside, one shy, the other bold, each in turn. I wanted to know everything about their life. How many lives did I pass by because I didn't ask the simple questions, "How, when, where," instead of just "Why?" "You're not asking me why we're in Bunia instead of Barcelona? I'm going to tell you even if you don't ask." Maïko started hating the sea. She'd spent ninety days in a skiff, and her mother had been eaten by a shark. In the Canaries, Maïko kept picturing pale corpses riding the waves. Anything but the sea, she decided, and Sayed agreed. They chose Africa because they feared the West that had little respect for their beliefs and customs. They moved to the very centre of Africa, as far from the tides as possible. "We got here in 2002. Two days before the war began. We bought the hotel, no, Maïko bought the hotel through one of her cousins who owned a Vietnamese restaurant in Kinshasa. What Kabanga did to those children is terrible. I could tell you, but it would have to stay between us. Kabanga is still just as dangerous."

What about the first kiss? Sayed blushed. It was on the beach. A kiss on the forehead. The second was on the cheek, at the hospital. I won't tell you about the third.

On the deck of the Bellevue, overlooking the bay filling with the sea and with it, peace and silence, I decided to save the world. Isabelle and Emma went by and smiled. A smile speaks. But I didn't answer.

I walked down the avenue de la Libération, went by the Café de la Paix, then past the United Nations offices to the market, ordinary in its poverty. Nothing was pretty there or worthy of admiration. Dust, car horns, kids selling mobile-phone cards and counterfeit Marlboros. Little slices of life. It's hard to explain, but those things delighted me, they reassured me, though the country, the city, the world filled me with despair. Yet one lived within the other. A unique, independent molecule didn't make me smile, though I was touched by a child smiling at me in this city I hate. How could I reconcile my visions of the world, tenderness and pain, lies and fervour, innocence and brutality?

I went back to the hotel and asked Sayed. Not the question – but questions.

"If you haven't found it by yourself, I'm afraid you never will. The answer is too simple: you have to love someone. Take Maïko and me. I understand why she can't stand the sea, the boat people, the beaches of the Canaries heaped with corpses. Maïko understands my nostalgia for the snow-covered mountains and she knows I dream of the sea that brought me to her. I know she misses Saigon, and she knows I dream of Mosul. We talk about it, we look at pictures, shows on TV, and we have tears in our eyes. If you only knew how we weep over this terrible world that brought us together and the two countries we had to leave. But in the end, we have to accept this twisted world because it brought us together, it gave us a house, a place to live."

Sayed got up to serve the customers, his eyes were misty, hardly the usual attitude of a Kurdish warrior. To love someone, what a stroke of luck, like an indulgence or a blessing that protects against sin and evil deeds, damnation and suffering, the way faith makes believers generous. But loving someone involves risk. I need to find my children. And run the risk of loving. I always think of the danger in love and never of the boldness. I'll start with Josué and the children.

49

The lizard was sleeping on my notebook. Myriam complained from her spot on the bed. "We're not doing anything here, we've just been bored stupid for three weeks. You never talk, you just think. You're not paying any attention to me. I'm going back to The Hague, I'll find a job as a translator, or a waitress." Carefully, I moved the lizard aside to keep from disturbing its sleep. The two of us have become fast friends. "Do what you want, Myriam." We have done everything there was to do in Bunia. We went for drinks at the Café de la Paix, we ate with the Lebanese who talked trafficking and deals, and we even went to the movies. The Bunia movie theatre! A large whitewashed room, a couple dozen plastic chairs, a cooler full of Primus, a big TV set perched on metal shelving probably pilfered from MONUC, and every film featured Jackie Chan or Sylvester Stallone. Then back to the hotel for a beer, with Vietnamese and Kurdish music trading places. Sayed and Maïko still in wonderment before this lousy world that brought them together, a place of stupidity and ignorance. They listened to BBC in the kitchen. They wanted to have children. We even went to the Sunday service led by Kabanga who received God's revelation in his cold prison cell in The Hague, a humid little box you wouldn't use to punish a dog. One night, warmth filled him, then a light appeared and a voice was heard, imperious and solemn. "You have sinned by the sword, but you will know redemption by the cross. The Hema people will dominate only if they follow the path of my word." The church dissolved in shouts of "Hallelujah" and "God bless the Hema." In the tent, all dressed in white the way he was, Kabanga's lieutenants lifted their arms heavenward, shouting, "Praise God," echoed in unison by the crowd. Myriam smiled. I felt like throwing up. We travelled to Lake Albert and ate a meal with some Canadians in the oil business. They were waiting for Kabanga to take over again. I thought of Josué. I'd heard nothing from him, but he was sending out rumours, according to Joseph.

Myriam wanted to live. What did that mean? She probably didn't know. But our mechanical lovemaking that was happening ever less frequently wasn't going to provide her with the illusion of living. "Do what you want, Myriam."

50

Myriam left me. At first I didn't notice. The more I think, the more I drink. In Africa the idle White man sits down in the sidewalk café to drink, then goes to the restaurant where he keeps on drinking. Not that he actually wants to drink; he wants nothing at all. I must have been sleeping while she packed her bags. Her leaving did not sadden me. Just another failure I should have foreseen. My life with the humans is a string of remarkable mistakes. I don't know how to love, or I lost the instruction manual. The results are the same. I'm alone and I'll never have a home of my own. Sayed thinks that my permanent state of intoxication is due to heartbreak. I haven't heard anything from Josué for a month and Joseph disappeared a few days ago. Madeleine is doing it with me for free, and she whispers sweet nothings in my ear in an ersatz of passion. The Lebanese guy finally understood I didn't want to invest in his dirty deals.

I've moved from Primus to whisky. Primus is like lead. It makes the body heavy, whereas whisky numbs me. I'm giving Madeleine a little money now, since she comes upstairs more often and she has three kids. She didn't complain when I gave her twenty dollars the first time, and neither did she thank me. She just smiled. She's nice, and I'm touched sometimes by her hopes both naïve and sincere in equal parts, but her eyes never really focus, and she laughs at everything and cries for no reason. I'm jealous. I have neither laughter nor tears. I can be sad and smile, but that's as far as I go. Sayed believes in destiny, and since I'm a good man, a good woman will surely appear, carried here by an unfurling oceanic wave that will deposit love upon our shore. I went back to Kabanga's Sunday service. His preaching has become less evangelical and more nationalist. His lieutenants have dropped the white robes and gone back to military camouflage.

I told Sayed about my idea for a French bistro. "The problem is the ingredients." Of course he was right. How would I find quality kidneys and Dijon mustard, hanger steaks and shallots, Toulouse sausages and duck breast? Those things were just memories of my father and a time when I knew what having a home meant.

Kabanga showed up at Sayed's restaurant and ordered fried rice and a Mutzig beer. His arrogant self-assurance got on my nerves, but I said nothing, and quieted the words in my head.

(I've been studying you for three years, Mr. Kabanga. I know you better than your wife does, the one who tried to kill you. I know how the rooms are arranged in your house, I know what you have for breakfast, and all your eating habits. I know the names of your tailor and your barber. I read your thesis on Hema alienation. I know about your agreements with the mining and oil companies, your deals with the Lebanese and the Rwandans. I could tell you how many ounces of gold and how many carats you've exported. The figures are in my room. I know that you stuck a lit cigar in a child's anus, and that the child is named Josué. I know everything about you, and I am here so you'll be judged for your crimes.)

It all stayed inside my head. I watched him eat and felt no pride. He offered to introduce me to some Rwandan friends to talk business. I said I'd think about it. I needed to talk to Marcel first.

"Who's Marcel?"

"My advisor, Mr. Kabanga."

I remembered, as I watched him go, that I never associated the title "Mister" with Thomas Kabanga.

A message from Josué, carried by the same little red-haired boy who this time asked for rice and of course a beer that he drank from the bottle like a real man. Mimicking a man, but with a child's laughter when I made fun of the way he imitated adults. He set his revolver on the table. "I'm not a child anymore. You need to answer, Mister."

"Everybody is here or almost. There's thirty of us or more. We have guns. We've been training. We shoot good, we're ready to move. We decided democratically to judge Kabanga and sentence him to death. You have to show us how to do a trial. We want to do it right. We want to judge before we kill him, judge the way you did in The Hague. You told me you wanted justice, you'll get it, and so will we."

"I'll come when you call." The kid ran off bearing my message. He forgot his revolver. He came back for it with a worried look. I held out the object he would probably use to perforate the lungs of some stumbling drunk who wouldn't give him a thousand francs or a woman coming back from the market after selling her manioc paste and a handful of tomatoes. A tomato salad. I'd go for a tomato salad and another whisky. Madeleine came and sat next to me. "You're not right, you're not right, how come not?" Sayed and Madeleine told me I was drinking too much and if I looked close enough, I'd see happiness right around the corner.

There was that young woman on the pebbly beach. Maybe happiness was there, an aperitif away. Too afraid to offer a Ricard to a pretty stranger who smiled at me. I really am useless. This was the hour when the sun slipped behind the first hill, and the noise became lighter somehow, the vehicles slower and the horns softer. Then someone screamed. I heard shouts, people rushed into the restaurant. I saw how the walls were more cracked than ever and everything smelled bad, sweat and oil and soybeans. The world stank. Sayed grabbed me by the arm and pulled me outside. Joseph's naked body lay there. A body missing its nose, its lips, and its penis. On his chest, his killers had painted a cross with his blood.

The lizard I have taken to calling Marcel watched me write an e-mail to a friend from the Court. "Kabanga tortured and killed Joseph. Do something, for Christ's sake."

The answer came back. "We can't do anything, Claude. Kabanga is the past for us. Good luck."

51

Marcel is sleeping with me now. He takes up position on Myriam's pillow, and when Madeleine comes, he goes and nests at the foot of the bed, patiently awaiting the end of our amorous theatrics. He reclaims his spot as soon as she leaves. I have a friend at last. I'm not a person with a heroic streak. Not that I'm afraid – I just don't have enough imagination about myself. Neither hero nor lover, an amputee from ordinary life, one of life's casualties.

52

Since Joseph's death, Sayed has been staying close to me. He wants to talk, I can feel it. He asked me if I'd heard the rumours. No, but I do know that here rumours are like the wind.

You know what that means. You know how the wind blows. You can't grasp it or take it into your hands and capture it, but it's all around, it envelops you and sometimes it slows you down. It rustles the leaves of quiet trees, changes the rhythm of a man who is walking, and who bends his back to push through the invisible force. In Africa, rumour is like the worst kind of wind, like a sandstorm. The wind goes where it wants to. No-one knows the origin of the wind of rumour, but it blows and chokes people, it makes them blind and mad. Sometimes, often, it kills and starts bloody conflicts. When Sayed told me about the rumours, he described ten versions that had the inhabitants fearful, and that set off new alliances, meetings, and negotiations. No-one knew where the rumour came from, but it had taken over the city. I wasn't just a rumour anymore, I was a fact that no-one understood, which made more rumours about me spring to life. I was responsible for Kabanga being freed, I had come to kill Kabanga, I had come to work with him because I'd lost my job at the Court, I was crazy for Black women, I was a pervert, I wanted to take over the town's economy. The importance I'd acquired did not make me happy. In every rumour lies a danger, and I was worried.

In the sandstorm that swept down the avenue de la Libération, in the three restaurants, the little bars in

173

private houses, people started talking about a new armed group. Supposedly it was made up of kids, and the chief was named Josué. Supposedly it had made an alliance with the Lendu to seek revenge against Kabanga.

The winds of rumour said they'd formed a camp near Bogoro. They were out to steal the gold, and traffic in diamonds, and reach Lake Albert that was running with oil. To tax the goods exported into Uganda, you had to control that little town where three roads meet, all leading to untold riches.

"My father used to say that you can't take the hatred out of hearts a century old. Here, every heart, even the child's, is a century old. They are fed on stories and fables and old wounds, and you can write a name on every scar. Sometimes it's the name of someone's family, but most of the time it's the name of a group, an ethnicity. You have to understand the importance of the tribe. It's what you call social security. The tribe is family and there's no such thing as justice. To make a long story short, Kabanga is getting ready to conquer what he'd lost, the Lendu are preparing their defence, and the children have formed an armed group that wants to kill Kabanga. Everyone knows you come from The Hague. We knew that before you got here. That's the way Africa is. You should leave. There's nothing good for you here. Please forgive me for speaking openly, but I consider you a friend and you seem so alone."

53

But at least I have Marcel.

54

Madeleine acted the perfect lover. She put aside her prostitute's chatter and trotted out her legitimate vocabulary. She kissed me sweetly like a woman in love. Of course we still fucked, but afterward, she stretched languorously, ran a finger along my cheek, planted a delicate kiss on my forehead, then talked about what we might do the next day, she called me mon amour and knocked on my door in the morning, she brought fruit and sometimes flowers. Madeleine was my occupation; she filled the void. That word doesn't frighten me. Her love, exposed that way, was an irritation. I took advantage, I exploited, I had my pleasure, I didn't think about it. On this torrid morning, she appeared. I hadn't slept all night, I stank of perspiration, I was running with it. She was carrying a platter and set it down on the bed. Two eggs, fruit salad, and real coffee, not Nescafé. Her smile said how proud she was, how she'd thought of everything and considered my pleasure. How could I tell her? There must have been a way that wouldn't hurt her but would free me from the discomfort that increased with each sweet caress that belonged to a woman really in love. "Thank you, Madeleine, but I don't love you. I feel friendship for you but nothing else." Then came the scalpel of honesty: "I'm just fucking you, that's all, I'm sorry." She screamed and yelled. I was the worst man she'd ever met, just another White exploiting the Blacks. I didn't answer. I watched Marcel. "And you never even made me come."

Then she left.

55

Brittany. I was thinking about Brittany as I ate a plate of rice that came from no particular country. Sayed explained how it worked. He and Maïko mixed their spices into the same dish. In other words, they made love in the kitchen as they added their Vietnamese and Kurdish flavours to the rice. The dish was scented with both lemon grass and cumin. Why Brittany? For the sea that fascinated me, the oysters, the faces scoured by the wind, but most of all for that moment that haunted me, Isabelle and Emma walking away from the deck of the Hôtel Bellevue, and me letting them go. I had stopped thinking of the children. I was thinking of myself. It was the first time in my life that I considered myself and neglected everyone else.

Sayed wanted me to go back home. He was worried, I could tell, for his own security. "I have no home, Sayed." Sometimes I dreamed of the Bay of Paimpol, but it was a sepia dream like a nostalgic photo lightly hued with sadness and regret for those smiles I never cared to follow.

The rumours were running full force. Kabanga had gotten weapons from the Chinese. The Congolese were obsessed with the Chinese, they'd replaced the Americans in the African imagination, standing for a confusion of fear and hope. The rumours roared. Kabanga had allied himself with the Canadian oil companies that were financing him.

Marcel has made himself very much at home, as if he were the rightful tenant. I need a plan. Four hours sitting in front of a piece of paper, and no rational idea, only fears, hopes, and feelings. I'm losing my way. I don't have a globe where I could find my position, and no expert accounts, no complex studies, just me and a country I know without ever experiencing it, a town that was keeping an eye on me, a hegemonic lizard, and old mistresses who inspire no regret.

At the cinema, I got a Primus, avoided people's stares born from rumours, and watched a completely infantile Stallone picture I'd seen three times before. Absolute emptiness can replace Prozac.

56

Josué sent for me. He must have needed me for something.

The driver Sayed found wanted three times the normal price to take me to Bogoro. Dieudonné's look was as trustworthy as a snake. He argued and improvised, the usual exchange between rich and poor. The road is dangerous, I'm White and that's not all, the Rwandans are out to get me, and besides, I raped Madeleine. He strung together the grains of sand from the storm of rumours. I had no answer to Dieudonné who was rumour incarnate. "You're a dangerous man, you understand" he concluded. "I'm married, I have children." No ring on his finger, but I had no choice. Very amusing. I managed a smile, at least in my head. I'm dangerous? All I have are a few ideas, and fewer dreams by the day. When I accepted his exorbitant demands, I realised my dreams were illusions, notions and nothing more, wind blowing through a deserted landscape.

"Hello, monsieur Claude." Josué had aged in these two months, not in his face or body, but in his cold eyes that gave lie to the smile he greeted me with. There were a dozen of them at the checkpoint, all little more than children. Josué pointed to a shelter made of branches and leaves that served as his headquarters. My children – what a ridiculous expression! – were taxing every vehicle that passed. Money, chickens, sacks of rice, and when a bush taxi stopped, Josué waved a girl out of the minivan. She was the sum to be paid at customs. She let herself be escorted into the shelter and sat down next to me. She didn't say a word, she didn't protest, as if being the ransom of men were part of her life. Josué played the boss. He gave orders, shouted at his men, hit them with the butt of his AK-47 when he felt he needed to. He was respected. The checkpoint business faded when the sun went down. A few minutes walking, and we reached what seemed to be the shadow of a camp. A few fires showed huts and tents made of UN tarps.

In the silence, we ate boiled manioc washed down with beer. Josué gave the girl to one of his comrades. She didn't protest; she followed him, her shoulders bent. The act wouldn't be classified as a rape because she didn't object. Josué lit a joint and passed it to me. I declined. He'd let his beard grow, maybe to make himself look older. His eyes wouldn't meet mine, but he gave orders in a firm voice, he threatened and cursed out everything and everyone as he ate his meal. A real boss. When childhood is stolen, so say the studies, the result is adult cruelty or teenagers who never grow up. "There's a hundred of us here." The humid heat and the smell of charcoal and eucalyptus made my head spin. The soft breeze caressed my skin and the whispering leaves reassured me, the way music calms the troubled soul. I said nothing, I waited, willing to witness Josué's transformation. His scars kept me from passing judgement. He was an authoritarian boss for his comrades, but a traumatized child for me. "More are coming every day. With the taxes from the checkpoint, we're buying weapons. We're going to do the justice you didn't." The court was almost ready. The kids in the camp were witnesses. "What about the lawyers?" I asked the question, but didn't believe in it. "The guilty don't deserve lawyers. And you know Kabanga is guilty." Yes, I do, I'm convinced without a doubt, that's why I'm here. "I'll be his lawyer." Josué looked at me like I'd fallen from the sky. "You want to double-cross us?" I said no. Everything involving a fair trial and the right of the accused to a defence was useless here. But I would defend Kabanga in Josué's court.

57

The children had style and audacity, imagination and courage. My children have tipped into the infinite labyrinth of vengeance. My children! They never were mine. I watched Josué giving orders, humiliating the lower ranks, strutting like a rooster. His story bonded him to me, not the person he was. At one time I loved him because, through his testimony, he contributed to the work of justice, my justice. His brand frightened me.

Josué described how they captured Kabanga. On Sundays, Kabanga held services, then received visitors, advised, counted the supporters, enrolled fighters, drafted the less willing, then he took a nap as he waited for the evening meal to be served. That was when the Hema elites showed up, with a few Rwandans and Lebanese, depending.

They discussed how the future riches would be divided when Ituri became an autonomous region, controlled by Kabanga's forces. They drank plenty as they planned the next war. On Sundays, Kabanga let his bodyguards drink and skim off what they could from the city. Sunday was sacred, a day of rest. The midnight attack on Kabanga's villa led by thirty or so child soldiers backed by Lendu fighters was just a formality. "They were drunk and snoring away." Josué was still enjoying the moment.

Kabanga acted superior and indifferent. He was an imbecile, totally self-absorbed. We ended up confined to the same cabin. He tried being friendly, and wanted to explain his cause. "Kabanga, you're a total shit." Out of principle, I was going to try and defend a total shit. I had to be the stupidest person on earth. Kabanga stopped talking to me. He sweated and wouldn't eat; he must have felt death's breath upon him. He wasn't praying since he'd sold his cross to a guard for three beers.

I knew the arguments for the defence, since I'd consulted the few pieces of evidence that might support him. I spelled them out and explained them, without much conviction. The judge found all that amusing. A self-appointed judge named Josué. He trotted out the witnesses, who were his comrades, other child soldiers, who told stories I knew. Kabanga started yelling and insulting them, he called them liars, then started crying, he kneeled down and called upon God, 'our God', and begged for forgiveness. A rifle butt to his temple silenced him. Blood poured from his nose.

"Now I want to question monsieur Claude from the International Criminal Court."

Josué put on the kind of smile that serial killers wear in the movies. I would be part of his vengeance.

"You know the accused very well."

"No, I don't."

"Didn't you write the report that got Kabanga accused when you were at The Hague?"

"I analysed the file and made recommendations to the prosecutor."

"You know the testimony that supports the accusations against Kabanga. Did you check their credibility?"

"Yes."

"On the basis of your analysis and this testimony, you recommended that Kabanga be tried for war crimes, right?"

"Yes."

I could guess the next question. I knew this was all just a parody; Kabanga was already dead. My answer, and I would not lie, would justify them in their own eyes.

"Monsieur Claude from the International Criminal Court, do you think that the accused before us is guilty of the crimes he's charged with?"

"Yes."

The children worked fast. A few minutes after I'd said, "Yes," I heard a burst of gunfire and shouts of joy. I retreated to my cabin as the children celebrated the event. Josué came in and offered me one of his girls. I want to sleep, Josué. I just want to sleep.

58

Sayed was very upset. The Vietnamese cheese was putrid and the beer warm. Sorry about the beer, he told me, then he described the latest rumours according to which I had ordered Kabanga's execution. "You'll stay inside and leave as soon as you can. Maïko and I like you well enough, but we don't want trouble and you're trouble. If you're a friend, you won't want to cause trouble for your friends." Of course, Sayed, I'm your friend and I'm going to leave. "There's a flight for Kinshasa tomorrow." Sayed really did want me to leave. I did too. I'd screwed up everything here. Actually, I never succeeded in anything.

I packed my bags. Maybe I'd find work in the capital. Marcel was sleeping on the pillow.

Why I slipped Marcel into my briefcase the next morning, I'll never know. A man has to be pretty lost to fall in love with a lizard. "You have to find your home." Those were Sayed's goodbye words.

In Kinshasa, a dozen policemen were waiting for me. I was accused of being an accessory to murder, but since the victim was Kabanga and I enjoyed the protection of the Minister of Justice, I was sentenced to be expelled from the country on the next flight to Paris. Only three hours separated Paris from Brittany. A home – you're right, Sayed, I need my own home. I'll get a room at the Bellevue and find that place. But the hotel and the restaurant had disappeared. The building had been turned into condos for rich vacationers. I used to have friends here, and I still have memories and regrets. They might make the foundations of a home. A few emotions on which I might start stacking stones, maybe even a mantelpiece.

I gazed at the Bay of Paimpol, and remembered those neglected smiles I'd missed. Here my house would stand. Sayed, I'll send you a picture when I find it.

59

And I did find a house. It's in Plouézec, five hundred metres from the sea that I can glimpse from my bedroom window. An old fisherman's dwelling with a small garden, and trees as old as the house. Mother would hate the furnishings, and she'd be right. But Marcel is getting along fine in the mists of Brittany. He spends all day outside, then comes in when evening falls to sleep on the free pillow. I got rid of the television. I don't have a computer anymore. I don't even read the papers. I look, I walk, I feel, I dream (I never dreamed before), and I imagine. I imagine life with a woman and children. I figure that's what it's about. It will come to me since I don't know how to find it.

I'm still writing in my notebooks. They accumulate, and I keep them for no reason I can think of. Yesterday, before the storm uprooted trees, blew tiles off the roof, and slammed the shutters I had neglected to close, I wrote, "I didn't ruin my life entirely, I got close, but not close enough." Then I lay down with Marcel and listened to the uproar.

60

After the storm blew through, the Arctic cold froze the trees and made the leaves shrivel on the branches. Houses in Brittany are not made for intense cold, and despite the fire crackling in the centuries-old hearth, I'm shivering. Five centimetres of snow followed the cold snap, covering the artichoke and bean fields. The harvest will be poor this summer. The birds are getting desperate. The insects have died of cold and the worms have sought refuge deep in the earth. The sea beats against the coast and rocks the fishing boats. A trawler sank. The grey sky is nearly black. I haven't seen Marcel for three days. I suppose Congolese lizards can't take a winter like this one.

Marcel is dead, and I'm sad. Tomorrow I'll buy a cat at the Paimpol pet shop. I think I'll call it Miou-Miou, like the actress from Brittany.

I don't want to die alone.

The Translator

David Homel is a writer, journalist, filmmaker, and translator. He is the author of six novels, including *The Speaking Cure*, which won the J.I. Segal Award of the Jewish Public Library and the Hugh MacLennan Prize for Best Fiction from the Quebec Writers' Federation. He has translated over a dozen French works, receiving the Governor General's Literary Award for Translation in 1995 and 2001. Born and raised in Chicago Homel currently lives in Montreal.

The Author

Gil Courtemanche (1943-2011)[1] was a journalist and novelist in third-world and international politics. Born in Montreal, he became a journalist on Radio-Canada (the French language part of the Canadian Broadcasting Corporation) in the early 1960s. After several years of reporting, hosting and commentating there he hosted the first public affairs magazine for Télé-Québec before returning to Radio-Canada and writing for Le Jour and La Presse. From 1986 he worked on progressive publications, wrote on international affairs and made television documentaries on the Rwandan genocide and AIDS in Africa, leprosy in Haiti, the politics of water, agricultural development in the Philippines, education for disabled children in Thailand.

Courtemanche is the author of ten books. The best known is *Un dimanche à la piscine à Kigali*, which documents the Rwandan genocide and which was made into a feature film, and which brought comparisons Camus and Greene. He died of cancer in 2011.

Seren Discoveries

Seren Discoveries is a series of translated literature which aims to introduce the reader in English to leading authors often writing in 'minority' languages or from 'peripheral' cultures. It includes works from Albanian, Basque, Québécois and Czech languages and from Francophone Haiti and Luxebourg. Future translations are planned from China, Greek and French.

Fiction

Fatos Kongoli: *The Loser*
Yannick Lahens: *The Colour of Dawn*
Kirmen Uribe: *Bilbao-New York-Bilbao*

Poetry

Petr Borkovec: *From the Interior*
Jean Portante: *In Reality*